"Break The Cycle"

Marquise T. Watson

You can Because you think You Can

Enjoy!

—Marquise

 BLUE MAGIC

BLUE MAGIC PUBLISHING INC.

www.bluemagicpublishing.com

Break The Cycle

Copyright 2010 by Marquise Watson.
All rights reserved.
Published by Blue Magic Publishing, Inc.,
Williamstown, New Jersey.

Book edited by: Sological Underpennings
For general information on our other products and services or for technical support, please contact our Customer Care Department at 888-237-6101 (toll-free/fax).

Watson, Marquise.
Break The Cycle / Marquise Watson.
ISBN 9780970791573
Library of Congress Control Number: 2010927474

"Break the Cycle"

Dedication

To my nana and my grandpa – I'm holding it down

To my moms – The good life is coming soon

To every kid who wants to live their dream –

You're in total control, go live it!

info@marquisewatson.com

Acknowledgements

First, I would like to thank God for putting me in the state of mind to even write this book and for giving me the patience and strength to see that it was completed. I want to thank my moms and pops for being supportive. My mother has been the biggest motivator for me. Special thanks go to my nana who insisted I write and finish this book. She had been telling me to write a book ever since I could remember and unfortunately she's not here to read it but I'm sure she would approve of the message that it contains. I want to thank my grandma for being an amazing grandmother to me and influencing a lot of things that helped me to write this book. I want to thank my grandfather for being the man he was. Even though he isn't here to see this, he is one of the main reasons I approach life the way that I do. I would like to thank my brother for his contribution to this book and for keeping my spirits up when I felt challenged. I know that together we will make a great impact on the entertainment industry. I would like to thank my sister for all of her help and for listening to all my ideas as I created the story. I would like to thank my entire family for their love and support. I would like to thank my friend Toyah B. for all the long hours we spent creating the structure and the tips you gave me for this book. Without you I would have been lost. I would like to thank Mr. and Mrs. Pettiford for giving me the opportunity to make my dream come true, for helping me and answering my million questions. I'm grateful for everything you two have done. I would like to thank the editing team for making this book what it is. I would also like to thank Reverend Branch for taking the time out of your busy schedule to meet with me. Your advice caused me to slow down and take things one step at a time. You told me that getting to where I want to be will be a journey and to choose one thing and accomplish that and then go on to the next. I started writing this book right after that meeting. I would like to thank my girlfriend for all the time spent helping me get everything right and for holding me down the way that you have. Thank you for believing in me, giving me words of encouragement and making the journey as fun as you have. I want to say thanks to my Facebook family for the encouraging words. Last, I would like to thank every person who told me that they were sick of reading all those novels about sex, money and drugs and that they wanted to read something more positive and real to give them inspiration. I hope that you find this book to be all that you hoped for. For anyone that I forgot to mention please know that I appreciate everyone who helped make this book possible. I'm living my dream and I hope you are living yours.

Chapter One

I woke up to work in another man's dream. Monday through Friday, my routine was the same: open the doors, clean the floors, do inventory, and make sure the place smelled pleasant. My labor helped another man make a fortune, while I was stuck making crumbs. When I returned home, my clothing stunk with pearberry, lavender and stagnation. I had been working at Victoria's Secret since the 11th grade.

Seems like an odd place for a man to work, right? Well, the job has its perks. I met busloads of beautiful women daily, the smell (which I carefully maintained) was so much better than warehouses, and the discount came in handy for my wifey, Lauren. What a beauty she is. You wouldn't believe how she took advantage of ya boy's employee discount. But hey, that's what I allowed.

Ten o'clock hit and it was time to open up. Ya boy is an expert womanologist: I pushed the push-ups, the perfume, and the lace. I had the thongs, the hip-huggers, the cheekies, the slips, and the babydolls; I taught her how to live, lounge, and love. What do you need: sports or convertible? Yes, fellas, they have bras just like the cars. And, did you know that about 44% of women in the world are B cups? Surprised the hell out of me.

Six Hours Later....

"Thanks for shopping at Victoria's Secret, have a good ni—-."
My customer didn't seem to notice, but my voice trailed off as a new girl approached the counter. She was bad: Reese's cup brown with short hair. Red, blue, and silver toe nail polish covered her pretty little toes, a nod to the 4th of July. Yes, she took care of her feet; was that a purple and yellow butterfly tattoo on her left foot? Her eyes put me in a trance and her lips were juicy like watermelon slices. Her red jeans looked painted on and a white tunic covered her well-sculpted upper body. She threw one of the new lingerie sets on the counter for me to ring up and then she spoke.
"Hey, can I have an application?"
"Baby, you're hired," I said immediately.
"Are you serious? Wait, so are you the manager?" she said giggling.
"Yeah, I'm the assistant manager, but sweetie, I'ma make sure you get hired. What's your name?"
"Tosha."
       I walked around the counter to get a little closer and make sure she got a hint of my cologne.
"Call me Mari. I peeped you earlier while I was in the food court. I was hoping you might make your way in here."
"Well, lucky for you, I needed some new lingerie," Tosha said.
"I wouldn't mind seeing you in this, mama. I'm sure your man would

love it," I said.

"I don't have a man so I'm gonna be the only one lovin' it."

"Oh good, that means I shouldn't have no one in my way then," I said.

"Nope, you got a clear lane playa, lay it up," she said with a bright smile on her face.

That statement let me know she was a bold one. I felt like a giant standing next to her. She had to be like 5'2, and I stand at 6'0, so she was looking up to me. Being so close up on her, I noticed her beauty mark on the left side of her cheek. On her neck, she had three tattoos: a heart, a butterfly, and a flower. Her nose ring made her even more desirable. The confidence she displayed was turning me on: it reminded me of my ol' lady.

I had her fill out the application and leave it with me. The store started to get busy and I didn't have time to get into a real conversation with her. I rang her up and gave her my number, hoping I would see her again.

"Ay Tosha, take my number down and hit me up sometime," I said. She pulled out her iPhone and keyed me in.

"Okay, Mari. I'll hit you up later."

I left work and went home. Most of my homies were out seeing the fireworks with their ladies. My lady was out of town so the only plans I had were to take a shower and play on my PS3.

As I stepped out of the shower, the phone rang.

"Hey Amari; it's Tosha. What's up?"

"I just got out the shower. What's going on?"

"I'm chillin', watching reruns of Bad Girls Club. You got anything planned for tonight?"

"Nah, I was just 'bout to lay down and play Madden," I said.

"Well you wanna come over and chill with me? I was thinking of watching the fireworks and getting some ice cream."

"Aight, no problem. Gimme a minute to throw some clothes on."

"Aight, take my address down."

"Aight, hold up let me get a pen."

I wrote down the address and thought about just staying with her in the house instead of going to see the fireworks. I wasn't trying to take that risk of people seeing me in public with this girl. If she had found out, Lauren would have killed me, but Tosha was so sexy. Besides, there's nothing wrong with a little friendly chill session. At least that's what I always told myself.

"Alright, I'll be there in a minute."

I hung up with shawty and threw on my favorite pair of cargo shorts: off-white colored with blue stitching. I threw on a red polo and some red chucks to complete my Independence Day look. Smells are very important when you're dealing with the opposite sex, so I had on my best cologne. Light-skinned brothers were out of style, so to capture these chicks' minds I needed to do more than flash a Colgate-smile. Once I felt the look was complete, I hopped in my whip and headed to Tosha's crib. Maybe it was the anticipation, but it felt like it took forever to get there.

Tosha's neighborhood was nothing like mine. The air seemed fresher, the sun seemed brighter, and the birds seemed to put more effort into their songs. Was that a rainbow? It was no house on the hill, but yeah, her home trumped my apartment building. While I shared hallways with meandering crackheads, the users in Tosha's neighborhood had the class to enjoy their cocaine in private. Her parents must have a little money.

By the time I walked up the steps, her door was already open. She must have seen me pull up. Out of courtesy, I pressed her doorbell and called out her name.

Tosha came down the stairs and ordered me to make myself at home in the living room. The inside of the house was even nicer than the outside. She had a big screen HDTV hanging on the wall, a nice L-shaped leather sofa set, and one of those soft rugs I've always wanted in my room. In my apartment all we had were wooden floors (but we kept them shining). Paintings covered the walls and she had a blockbuster Blu-ray section. The mood suggested by the lit fireplace did not scream "friendly chill session."

"Hey Mari, you got here just in time," Tosha said as she sat on my lap.

I wrapped my arm around her waist and asked, "Why you say that? What you got planned for me?"

"Well, the fireworks are about to start soon," Tosha said.

"Oh okay. Where are they?" I asked.

"Not too far," she answered as she grabbed me by my hand and escorted me into the kitchen.

On the counter were two fully-loaded sundaes: vanilla ice cream, covered with chocolate syrup, nuts, whipped cream and chopped strawberries on top. We grabbed our sundaes and headed out to her backyard. She had a swimming pool and a huge deck surrounded by chairs and rose bushes. It was everything I had dreamed of having for my family.

"We're here," Tosha said. We placed our sundaes on the dining table as we sat on the patio chairs.

"Oh word? You can see the fireworks from your house?" I asked.

"Yup, you can see them real good too. This way we don't have to deal with all the people," Tosha said.

Wow, did this chick just read my mind? I began to like her even more. We sat there, ate our sundaes, and enjoyed the fireworks. We talked and got to know each other better. She was a preacher's daughter, a biology major, and her moms worked for Rutgers University (the same school my sister just got accepted to). We had a good vibe, and I don't know why, but this year the fireworks seemed a little better than before (as if they were in HD or something). Maybe it was the intimate space, the beautiful girl sitting next to me, and the great connection we were making. After the fireworks were done, we headed back into the house.

"Ay Tosha, where your parents at?"

"They went to Paris to celebrate their anniversary," Tosha said as she put the dishes into the dishwasher.

"Oh that's wassup. I plan to go there someday, myself."

I grabbed the remote to turn the TV on. "Ay Tosha, you mind if I catch the rest of this baseball game? The Yankees are playing and you know I gotta watch my boy A-Rod."
"Yeah, go ahead. I'll be right back," she said as she walked upstairs.

I sat there watching the Yankees murder the Red Sox. I loved when the Yankees played the Red Sox because I knew my Facebook account would be going crazy with statuses talking about the game. I got on my Blackberry and rubbed the victory in the face of all my friends and reminded them that the Yankees were the best team in the league—not the Sox. As soon as I put my phone back on my holster, I saw the most scrumptious looking thing I had ever seen in my life. It was Tosha, in a way I had imagined but ten times better. She stood there in the lingerie she had purchased earlier that day. It was red, bright and confident just as she was. The way her breasts sat in the cami made me wonder whether the stitching was about to bust. Her thighs looked glossy: it was like she had used a whole bottle of baby oil. She licked her lips as if to add shine to spots her lip gloss might have missed. She walked up to me and struck a pose.
"Hey Mari, what you think?" Tosha asked.

I stood in a bit of a trance, admiring her body. It was like seeing a beautiful butterfly on a sunny day as it flapped its wings and demonstrated the freedom we all wished we could have physically, mentally, and spiritually.
"Oh, umm, I love it, I actually feel over dressed," I replied while gazing

at her legs.

"Well, take off them shorts, baby; the night is still young," Tosha demanded.

I didn't wanna do it. I had a beautiful wifey, (a good wifey at that). I promised myself I wouldn't cheat on Lauren again, but Tosha was irresistible. The lane was wide open, and I had to lay it up. Besides, I didn't wanna leave her disappointed.

One Hour Later....

It was done. She went to her stereo and turned on Drake's Best I ever Had. I laughed and took the song as a not-so-subtle "thank you." I loved it when women stroked my ego.

"Mari, hold me like I'm your wife. I just wanna be held, baby," Tosha yearned out loud.

I wasn't the type to cuddle with my hoes, but this girl seemed different; there was something about her. I held her in my arms as I soaked in the essence of it all. Moments went by, and I saw my Blackberry flashing; it was Lauren. She texted a smile, the letter "I," a heart, and the letter "U." I replied "ditto."

Although I felt bad, I convinced myself it was only one night. It was just like every other time; nothing was gonna come out of it. At the end of the day, no matter how many other women I smashed, my heart was with Lauren Hall.

Tosha offered me food; I declined. I wasn't really hungry, and I was somewhat tired. As we lay there under her covers, her head on my chest, I silently said my prayers and thanked God for this unforgettable Fourth of July night.

Chapter Two

During the week that followed our "chill session," Tosha and I shared small talk over text messages: nothing too heavy, though. Tosha was special, but she wasn't wifey.

It was Saturday morning and I woke to the savory aroma of breakfast. Scrambled eggs, crackling turkey bacon, bubbly cheese grits and the scent of sweet cinnamon rolls filled the house. I had slept at Lauren's place because she felt like we were losing our spark. We hadn't spent quality time together for what seemed like years to her, but really it had only been a few weeks. She was very much into romance. The night before, after dinner at her favorite restaurant, we played Scrabble, and finished the night cuddled up under the sheets, dozing off to a chick flick. I think it was called "The Notebook" or "The Scrapbook," something like that.

I walked into the kitchen. "Morning, sweetie. Breakfast smells good."

Lauren swore she was the next Rachael Ray. "Yeah, I know, and it tastes even better."

"After we eat I got something planned for us to do," I told her while eating the last piece of bacon on my plate.

"What you got planned for us?" Lauren asked.

"I want us to take some pictures. It's been a while so let's go and do that. When we're done, we can hit up Arcade Mania and be kids for a little bit."

"Oh wow, babe, we haven't been there since our first date," Lauren said sprinkling some pepper on top of her scrambled eggs.

"Yeah, it has been a while," I said.

"Do you remember what day that was?" Lauren asked.

"Baby, how in the hell am I supposed to remember the day we went on our first date? All I know is I was 18, and it was around the time I was going to prom."

"Uggh. Babe, you don't remember nothing do you?" Lauren said.

"I remember our anniversary and that's all that matters, honey."

I was 18 and just about to graduate when I met Lauren. She was 20, and in her second year of college. We were both from the hood. She graduated from the all-girl high school in a neighboring town and I went to the local high school in my city. I used to see her jogging around the track every Saturday morning while I was out shooting ball. She was built like a video dancer: not too skinny, but with a slim waist and a little junk in her trunk. She was so well proportioned. Usually a girl would either have a lot of ass, or a lot of breasts, but God blessed her with a little bit of both.

She looked so mature. At first I was a little hesitant to approach her, but eventually I went over and broke the ice; I couldn't let her get away. She had a different swag. While at that time most girls were wearing weave ponytails, micro braids, or some sort of tracks, she wore her hair pressed, tied up in a ponytail or laying down on her shoulders. It was never over the top and I fell in love with her look. She was a woman who embraced her God-given beauty. She felt no need to wear fake nails, or wear make-up, or even lip gloss for that matter. She actually used the same type of lip balm as me. It was a little strange to me but that's what made me fall in love with her.

Lauren was the best of both worlds. She was from the hood, so she understood the hood, but at the same time she didn't act hood. That's why I think we meshed so well together. She appreciated that I was cut from the same cloth as her, but she never had to worry about rival gangs coming after her to get to me, or worry about me getting locked up for pushing weight, or any of the other unnecessary things that some other girls had to worry about because of their boyfriends. She knew she had a thorough black man who was trying to figure life out and become a better man with each passing day. But we had our problems like everyone else. No relationship is ever perfect.

"Mari, why didn't you tell me you wanted us to take pictures; you didn't give me a chance to get my hair done."

"Babe, it looks good the way it is; don't worry about all that."

I helped Lauren clean up the dishes from breakfast. I used to always hear that a man would most likely marry someone who is like his mother and Lauren definitely reminded me of my mom. From her soul food that hit the spot every time, to her calm spirit, to her belief in God and her heartwarming personality, my lady had it all.

"Mari, which outfit do you like best: this purple and white sundress or these capris with this green halter top?"

"You know I love how you look in that purp, so throw on the dress. I'ma throw on this white and purple Nike T-shirt with some cargos and some purple chucks."

We got dressed and headed to the mall to take pictures. Luckily for us we didn't have to wait too long to take them. Normally, on a Saturday afternoon the Y.I.G Photo Studio was crowded, but we lucked up today. We took the 5x7 package that came with two poses. We would get two 5x7s, four 4x6s, and twelve wallets. That was just enough to divide amongst our families. For the first pose, I kneeled on one knee as if I was proposing. I have to admit, the thought of marriage did come across my mind sometimes, but that was only after watching them chick flicks with her or after she had just blown my breath away with her lovemaking. For the second pose, I held her chin with the tips of my fingers and we shared a light peck for the camera. I loved taking pictures. For some reason I felt like a star whenever someone snapped a flick of me. While Lauren talked with a friend, who happened to be waiting to take pictures with her boyfriend, I chatted with the photographer.

"Ay man, when did you get into this photography stuff? I see you have a real passion for it."

"Man, I fell in love with the camera when I was about ten years old," he told me while changing the backdrop for the next group of people.

"Oh, you was a youngin."

"Yeah, my father used to take me hiking and I would love to stand there and take pictures of the wild deer, the butterflies, the trees and the rocks. The whole natural scene was really exciting to me."

"I feel you. Well, your work is good, man. Keep doing ya thing."

"Thanks, man. I appreciate it," the photographer replied before calling the next group of people in.

Lauren and I hit up a couple of stores while we waited for the photos.

"Amari, let's go to Elegance."

"La La, I ain't trying to be in this store too long; you know how you get."

"We're not. I just want to look at these new totes."

Elegance was a store that sold bags and shoes. After being in there for about twenty minutes, and seeing her pick up bag after bag and shoe after shoe, I said, "Lauren, just pick the bag you like the most and I'ma get it for you."

"Mari, I can't get a bag without getting some shoes."

"You know what, get the shoes, Lauren. Matter fact, get them red pumps right there."

I had a fetish for seeing her in some heels, and she didn't have any red ones. I didn't know what it was, but she looked sexy as hell with them and her little freaky fishnets.

"Babe, you so nasty," Lauren said.

"Just hurry up, girl."

"Thanks babe. You know I love you, boy."

"I love you too, girl. Now come on. Let's go get our pictures before you find something else you want."

We headed back to Y.I.G Photo Studio and the pictures were ready. We opened the envelope and were very pleased.

"Aww, baby, they came out perfect," Lauren said smiling.

The pictures came out just how I had hoped they would. I gave a tip to the photographer and we headed to destination number two: Arcade Mania. All the games a man-child could possibly want were there, so we planned to devote several hours to playing ourselves back through our teenage years.

"Ay La La, what you wanna do first?"

"Let's go race on the track with the go karts."

"Babe, you don't want none of this here. You already know I'm nice behind the wheel."

Lauren and I got in line at the race track and ended up standing behind Tosha and another guy that I guessed was her date.

"Hey Amari, what are you doing here?" Tosha said, looking surprised to see me.

"I'm here enjoying the day with my lady. Lauren, this is Tosha. Tosha, this is my lady Lauren."

They exchanged phony greetings: "Hi, nice to meet you."

"So Amari, what's up with the job? When your manager gonna call me in for an interview?"

"I got you. The hiring manager went over the applications this week so he should be calling you soon. One of the girls working there just

quit so I'ma make sure you get her spot."
"Okay, don't forget me."
"I'm not gonna forget you."

Lauren's eyes never left Tosha's and vice versa. They were staring each other down like two boxers at a weigh-in. Finally we got into our go karts and started the race. Tosha made sure she bumped me; I guess that was a subliminal message to let me know she wanted to relive last weekend. She was good with her subliminals.

Although it was typical for me to juggle multiple women, this was the first time I landed in the dreaded face to face scenario. There I was in between the most beautiful woman I had ever seen and the woman of my dreams. I played it cool, and I made sure my girl knew that she ain't have to worry about Tosha (even though Tosha was giving me looks like she wanted me to pull the go kart over and get down with her right there on the track). We finished our laps around the track and me and Lauren went our separate ways from Tosha and her dude. A few hours went by and we enjoyed our time at the arcade. We played air hockey, laser tag, and many other games. Lauren enjoyed herself, and as far as I could tell, she didn't let the situation with Tosha affect her attitude. When we got in the car, I asked her whether she had fun. Her response wasn't quite what I expected.
"Yeah Mari, I had a good time. Let's go to the clinic."
"The clinic? Why you want to go to the clinic right now?"
"We haven't been in a few months: that's all. And it's time for our

checkup."

"So you want to go right now: like this second?"

"YES, I want to go now: like right now."

That's how my girl was. I knew the only reason she wanted us to go get checked was because she didn't like the way Tosha was looking at me. But instead of making a big scene or anything of that nature, she slickly suggested we go get tested. It had been several months and who was I to say no? The drive over to the clinic was quiet. We didn't talk much. I didn't know if it was because I had just bought that new Fresh Moss album, and she wanted to listen to it, or if she was feeling some type of way about what had happened at the arcade. Either way it was extremely quiet. It took us about a half hour to arrive at the clinic. We signed in and waited for the workers to call us in individually. I grabbed an ESPN magazine from one of the tables and read a few articles. Lauren read one of the parenting magazines. I hoped she wasn't getting any ideas because I was not ready to have no baby. I damn sure couldn't afford to have one.

"Amari Crews," the nurse called out.

I followed the nurse. Rooms in the clinic always seemed to be cold.

"How are you doing today, Mr. Crews?" the nurse asked.

"I'm doing quite well. And yourself?"

"I'm doing fine. Do you have anything to tell me before we start?"

"Anything like what?" I asked.

"Have you had unprotected sex since the last time I saw you here?"

"Unfortunately, yes, I have, but only one time with one girl. The other girls I strapped up on."

"Now, Amari, you know one time is all it takes."

"Yeah, I know, but I didn't have any on me and the mood was just so perfect."

"Mr. Crews how perfect do you think the mood would be if you contracted AIDS from this young lady or if you got this young lady pregnant?"

"You right, Ms. Ellen."

She took my blood and I pissed in a cup. We talked another ten minutes or so and she told me stories of people she knew who had made some of the same mistakes I made. As the conversation ended, she threw me a couple of gold raincoats and told me to protect myself. She said someone would call me within a week or so to let me know my results. Lauren was already done by the time I got out.

We pulled up to her house and before she got out she grabbed my hands and looked into my eyes.

"Amari, baby, you know I love you right?"

"Of course I know you love me. Why you ask that?"

"I want you to move in. We been together four…." I cut her off.

"Baby, you know how I feel. I don't want us to rush into anything."

"I'm sick of you saying that, Amari! I mean what are we rushing into? We been together four years, Amari. Four years going on five!"

"Listen, Lauren. I really don't want to get into this."

"You know what, Amari? You better figure out what you want to do with this relationship, and figure it out quick. I'm sick of being here alone, Amari."

I didn't bother saying another word. I loved my girl, but I was not ready to take that next step of moving in with her. I didn't have the finances to fully take care of her. I knew we had been together for four years, but it just wasn't the time. She was mad so I figured I'd keep quiet and let her cool off. I wasn't the type to argue with a woman. Real men just don't do that.

"Goodnight, La La. I love you. I'll text you when I get in the house."

"I love you too, Amari." She slammed the car door.

Chapter Three

A few days went by, and after a hard day of dealing with annoying customers, I went to pick up my sister from choir rehearsal. I arrived early and bumped into my pastor.

"Hey, Rev, what's going on?"

"Hey, Amari, everything is going well. How are your mom and grandmother doing?"

"They're doing good. And how is Mrs. Wilson?"

"She's just fine. I didn't see you last week, what happened?"

"Yeah, I know. I got caught up with work, but I'll be here this Sunday."

"Okay, I expect to see you."

"I'll be here, but what's going on with your Red Sox? Ya'll stink this year."

"We just going through a little slump right now. We'll be fine."

"A little slump, huh? You need to pray for them," I said laughing.

We shared a laugh and he went into his study to do whatever it is that pastors do. My sister came out of rehearsal surprised to see me there.

"Hey, brother. What you doing here?"

"I figured I'd pick you up since I just got off and ma's not feeling too well."

"Oh, what's wrong with momma?"

"She didn't tell me, but you know it's probably that job. I told her she needed to just quit and open up that babysitting business she always wanted. She got the certificates already."

"You know she scared. She gonna be stuck at that job until she retires," Sharea said.

"Yeah. I'm starving. Did you eat? Are you hungry?" I asked getting into my car.

"Nah, I didn't eat yet. Can we go get something from White Castle?"

"Yeah, I'm fiendin' for a vanilla milkshake right now, myself."

I saw a cherry red Honda Accord with a Zeta Phi Beta sticker on the bumper as I was ready to pull off. It was Nikki: another one of the ladies I fondled with on a whenever-I-felt-like-it basis. She was a beauty, not as sexy as Tosha, but she was in my starting lineup. We were real cool. I called her my model chick. She had flawless skin the color of sweet potato pie and long dreadlocks that were dyed different colors every time I saw her. That night her hair was an inky black. Even though she was slim she had more curves then a Blackberry. When she wore heels, she stood at about 5'9. Her hair and nails were always tight because she's a go-getta. She promoted parties for this crew called P.A.B (Party and Bullshit). She was one of them hood divas. She was classy, but if you tried to disrespect her, she let that 7th Street Projects lingo come out of her.

"Amari, wassup boo?" Nikki asked as she approached my car.

"Ay sweetie, wassup?" I said.

"I texted you the other day. Why you ain't reply back?"

Yeah, I got her text, but she wasn't wifey. Wifey was the only one that got replied to ASAP. She was just Nikki: simple as that.

"Oh, my inbox must have been full, because I never got it. What's going on? What you doing over here?"

"I'm just grustling, boo. Came over to pick up some money from my homegirl. You already know. I was trying to get up with you, though; we ain't spent no time together in a while. Tell your girl to give you the key to them handcuffs."

"Yeah, it has been awhile since we kicked it. Let's do something this weekend."

"Ok, how about Saturday? I'm throwing a passion party and I could use help setting things up."

"Cool with me. Just hit me up."

"Ok, I will. Just answer your damn phone."

"Relax ma. I got you." I said with my sexy grin. She gave me a kiss on the cheek and strutted across the street.

My moms had just told me that my sister had a male friend she was all head over heels with so it was time I ask my sister about this dude.

"So, Sharea, who is this Dante guy ma been telling me you all crazy about?"

"Dante is my boo-boo stank-stank," she said beaming.

"Whaaateevvaa. Ok, how old is Dante?"

"21," she said reluctantly.

"21. Ok, too old. So how did you meet him?" I asked turning the volume on the radio down.

"His cousin goes with one of my friends and they hooked us up."

"Well, what does he do Sharea? Is he in school? Does he work? What he doing with his life?"

"He's looking for a job now."

"So how's his job hunt going? It shouldn't be that hard for him to get a job. There are plenty of labor jobs out here, even in this economy," I said.

"He's been locked up before so it's kind of hard for him."

"He's been locked up?"

"Yes, and you know how hard they make it on people who come home from jail."

"Save the excuses, Sha. If he wanted a job he would have one. So I'm guessing he's not in school either."

"He's not in school; he's on his grind trying to become a rapper. He's good too, Amari. You should hear him. I think you would like him."

"A rapper, huh? Yeah, him and every other kid that can't play a sport."

"Amari, you not trying to become a rapper. Matter fact, what are you trying to become?" She took her glasses off to wipe them clean.

"Sharea, you know what I mean. Stop trying to be smart."

She was mad, but I didn't care. I did not want my baby sister dating no thug. I didn't care how nice he was, how cute he was, or how good he rapped. It was not going down: not with Sharea Monique Crews. I gave her a hard time, but truthfully my sister was what I would call any guy's dream girl. She was active in church and one of the top students in her high school's graduating class. She was in shape: not skinny, but not fat, either. She had golden brown skin that sparkled like diamonds, and she had a classy sense of style that was beyond most girls her age. She deserved someone much better, but she did have me thinking. Here I was questioning the plans of another young man and I didn't even have my own plans in order. I had become stagnant. We pulled up to the White Castle drive-thru.

"Would you like to try our new pulled pork sandwich?" the woman asked over the speaker.

"Nah."

"Welcome to White Castle. Can I take your order?"

"Yeah, I'll have three fish with cheese, two cheeseburgers, an order of fries and a vanilla milkshake."

"Sha, what you want?"

"I want a number four with a Sprite."

"Does that complete your order, sir?"

"Nah, I want a number four, with a Sprite and put some hot sauce, tartar sauce and ketchup in the bag."

"OK, your total is $15.86."

There were several cars in front of us, so as we waited for the food, Sharea talked on the phone with a friend and I thought about what I was gonna say to my little sister. My sister was my heart. I thought about the days we spent playing basketball together at the park; I remembered the nights we watched Who Wants to be A Millionaire and guessed the answers together. I reflected on how she looked like a lady in her prom dress this year. She was growing up so fast, and now she was 18 years old getting ready to be a college girl.

"Sha, tell your friend you gonna call her right back. We need to talk."

She did one of those big sighs (one of those sighs you do when your mother tells you to come here after you just got settled in your bed).

"What we got to talk about, Mari?"

"We need to discuss your lack of good judgment. I don't get it. I really don't get what you can possibly see in this Dante dude."

"Amari, he is very sweet. He's got a bangin body and he is sooo sexy."

"I don't care how sexy you think he is; it's not all about the look, Sharea. You don't need to be involved with someone like him."

"Mari, you don't even know him. You didn't even give him a chance."

"I don't know him; you right. But you don't know him either. All you know is his name is Dante and he wants to be a rapper. But what if that don't work out? What's his plan?"

"I don't know, but he's really good at rapping."

"Sha, you know how many people are good at rapping? Does he have any business knowledge? There's more to rap than rapping; the music industry is a business. Do you know anything about his past? You said he went to jail; what did he go to jail for? Matter fact, he went to jail, so that tells you right off the bat that he doesn't know how to handle himself."

"Mari, you don't even know what he went to jail for."

"OK, Sha, tell me. Tell me what I already know."

"He had a gun on him and a couple bags of weed; it isn't like he killed somebody."

I grabbed our food from the drive-thru attendant and continued to drive home.

"Sharea, listen to yourself. You are dating a young boy who smokes weed and carries guns. I can't believe you. I really can't believe you."

I couldn't believe that my little sister, who was going to college in just a few months, was giving this clown the time of day.

"I can change him, Mari; all he needs is a little support. He didn't have a father growing up or a male figure to really look up to so he's struggling with trying to find himself as a man.

"Sharea, did you forget that we didn't have our fathers either? That is not an excuse. As people we know right from wrong, and from what you telling me, your dude is all wrong and he ain't right for you."

There was a brief silence. Sharea turned her head and stared through the car window.

"Tell me this, Sharea; what do you want to get out of this relationship?"

"I really like him. Hopefully one day we can get married, have kids and live a good life."

"OK, that sounds all well and good. I want the same thing one day, but how on Earth could you consider having a husband who's in jail?

You might be signing up to have a baby daddy because he

probably gonna leave you as soon as he impregnates you."

"Amari, how could you say that? Everyone isn't like our fathers, Mari," she said cutting me off.

"I'm not saying everyone is, but what I am saying is a man don't really feel like a man unless he got his stuff in order; you hear me? And from what you telling me he doesn't even have a process to get his life in order. Why you think your little friend's baby's daddy is just that: a baby daddy? Why you think the cowards that lay down with you women get ya'll pregnant and as soon as the baby come, and they feel that heat, they haul ass? It's because they don't have no morals, no sense of responsibility, and no plans. But you girls fail to see that and then y'all get caught up in ya'll situations. You see it every day, Sha. This isn't new. And you need to understand that the decisions you make now will stick with you forever. So if you gonna be out here dating you need to date a dude that's on your level and you always need to think ahead and ask yourself if you could do better."

"Big bruh, I can say the same about you. I see the girls you be bringing by the house. You doing Lauren so dirty, Mari. That girl has been down with you since you were my age. How could you cheat on her? How could you say you love her and then sleep with Tosha or Nikki or Nicole or Shanika or Tonya? That isn't love, Mari. And what would you do if one of them got pregnant and chose to keep the baby? You gonna leave Lauren to be with them? No, you not. You just gonna be another baby daddy just like the dudes you trashing. So what are you doing with your life, huh? What's your plan? I know you not gonna be assistant manager at Victoria's Secret your whole life."

We pulled up to our apartment building, and at that very moment, I realized that I wasn't being a good example for my sister. I expected her to be this respectful classy young lady that made good decisions, but I was being the total opposite. Besides that, I had yet to figure out the road I wanted to go down in my own life, so who was I to question another man? I did have dreams of owning my own lounge someday, but that dream seemed so distant. My sister was right, and I couldn't do anything but agree with her.

"I don't know what I'm gonna do, Sharea, but I'm not feeling this. I ain't feeling it at all."

"I really like him, bruh, and I'm not leaving him. We're going to be fine so just leave it alone, okay?"

It pissed me off but what could I do? My sister was 18 and she was gonna do whatever she wanted to do. I couldn't stop her. I couldn't be around her every minute of the day so I put it in God's hands and asked that He protect her and help her smarten up.

"Sharea, I'm staying with Lauren tonight so tell mommy I'll be back tomorrow."

I made sure my sister got inside the building and headed over to Lauren's. I wasn't in the best of moods and Lauren always knew how to help me take my mind off of things.

Saturday came. I woke up, got fresh, and headed to Earl's to get my hair cut. Nikki had texted me while I was in the shop and said she wanted me to be at her crib around 3pm to help her set up for her little nasty freak party. When I arrived, her place was looking like the back of Spencer's. Her living room was in all red décor: red blinds, red furniture, and on a black table was all the paraphernalia. She had everything: marble dildos, metal handcuffs, door swings, position books, multi-flavored exotic love oil, and edible panties. The ambience was incredible. In tight booty shorts and a cami, she had my mind blown.

"Nikki, Nikki, Nikki, you look delicious."

"Thanks boo. You like what I threw on?"

"Do I? I'm ready to rip it off" I said pulling on her shorts.

"Amari, you gonna have to wait awhile before you get to these goodies. Just let me finish the macaroni salad, OK?"

"Alright, hurry up girl."

Nikki was so exciting. Having sex with Nikki was like smashing a Victoria's Secret model. She did her thing in the kitchen while I watched ESPN. My phone started ringing.

"Hello, may I speak to Amari Crews?" the woman's voice asked.

"I am Amari Crews; who is calling?"

"Hi Amari, this is Jackie from the clinic. Just to verify that I'm speaking to the real Amari Crews can you call out your id number? It is on the card you received from us."

I reached into my back pocket to pull my wallet out and get the card.

"It says W112F3."

"OK, Mr. Crews, I am sorry to inform you that you have chlamydia."

"Chla what?" I said. My jaw dropped, and for a second I think my heart stopped. What the hell did I get myself into?

"Chlamydia. It is a very common disease and can be easily treated."

"How do I get rid of it? I need to get rid of it ASAP."

"You are more than welcome to come down to the clinic so we can give you the medicine for it," Jackie said.

"OK, when can I come?" I asked.

"We open up at 9 am on Monday," Jackie answered.

"OK, I will be there at 8:45. Thank you."

"No problem. See you Monday, Mr. Crews."

My thoughts were scattered: I couldn't believe I had chlamydia. I felt so dirty, so disgusted with myself. I started to think of all the women I had sex with: there was Natalie from the North side, Shonda from around the corner, two Moniques (one from the Mall and the other from the movie theater), Tosha from the store, and Nikki.

Damn, I didn't know which one I got it from. Tosha was the only one I didn't strap up on, so I figured it must be her. Then again, maybe it wasn't Tosha. I done smashed so many chicks I couldn't even remember. Some I didn't even smash; some was just a quick oral. Damn I didn't strap up on my wifey either: shit, shit, shit. What if my girl has it? She is going to kill me. All four years of our great relationship are going to be down the drain. She would never forgive me for cheating on her, let alone for giving her a STD. I tried to stay calm around Nikki but my nerves were shot.

"Amari, what's wrong? Why are you sweating and pacing around?" Nikki asked.

"Oh, nothing, it's nothing. I'm just a little anxious about your goodies, that's all."

"Relax, boo. Save that energy for me," Nikki said.

I was out of it. Before I knew it, my shirt was already off, and I was unbuckling my belt. Nikki had stripped all of her clothes off. She laid on the sofa with one leg up and the other dangling to the floor. She had boxes of condoms, which were party favors for later. She took a condom out the box and proceeded to open it up.

"Amari, you need help with that belt?" she asked.

"Nah, I'm good, babe," I said.

I put the condom on, but I wasn't feeling right. My mind wasn't in it. As she grabbed me to insert me inside her, I paused.

"Whoa, whoa, hold up Nikki," I stopped.

"What's wrong boo?"

"Sorry, Nikki, I got to get out of here. I'll explain it to you later." I put my pants, shirt, and shoes back on and rushed out of her house.

"Wait, wait, Amari, don't go," Nikki pleaded.

"I got to go. I'll call you later. I promise."

Nikki sat there in total shock: mouth wide open. This was probably the first time a man had walked out on her while she was butt-ass naked. As I power-walked to my car, my stomach twirled and my heart raced. All I could think of was Lauren. How could I be so foolish? How could I cheat on Lauren? She had been with me through so much. She's my baby, my love, and my everything. I sat in my car punching my steering wheel. People walking by must have thought I was crazy because the more I punched the more the horn went off.

The phone rang and broke me out of my tantrum; it was Lauren. I already knew what was to come out of this conversation. Life as I knew it was over; the clinic had called her and told her she had chlamydia. She knew I gave it to her, and now she was calling me to end the relationship. I answered hesitantly, "Hey La La. Wassup, babe?" I said softly.

"Hey boo, what's wrong? Why you sound like that?"

I didn't want to tell her over the phone. I preferred to do it in person. "Nothing, nothing's wrong," I answered.

"OK, I was just calling to let you know the clinic called me."

My heart dropped. I felt a drip of sweat coming from the side of my head.

"I'm clean; they said I didn't have A.I.D.S. or any other STDs, as I expected."

I was ecstatic. I couldn't believe it. "Thank You, Lord" was all I could say to myself.

"Oh, okay babe. I figured that."

"Did they call you yet?" Lauren asked.

"Yeah, actually the lady just called me before you called. Everything is cool," I said.

I had to lie. I was happy that she didn't have anything, and there was no need for me to ruin her day by telling her about my mishaps.

"Oh okay. Well, I'm going out with the girls tonight to a movie. Are we going to church tomorrow?"

"Yeah, I told Reverend Wilson I would definitely be there."

"Okay, so come pick me up in the morning before you go," Lauren said.

"Aight, and call me tonight when you get in from the movies so I know you got home safe."

"OK boo. Mwah."

"Mwah"

Whoa, I was so relieved. My father had died from A.I.D.S., and I thought about how foolish I had been. I was acting just like the man I hated. He did the same thing to my mother as I was doing to Lauren, and that's why I never had a relationship with him. It was time to do what I should have done a long time ago. I sent a text message to each girl that I messed with on the side. It read, "Hey sweetie, I have enjoyed the moments we've shared but you deserve better. I feel that I should be a better man to my lady, so I can no longer take part in those lustful acts of our past. I know you will understand and I hope we can remain friends- Mari."

They all were cool women, so I doubted any of them would do anything bizarre like bust the windows out my car or anything. At least I hoped not. I decided to contact Sprint and get a new phone number. It was time I cut ties from my past.

Chapter Four

My grandmother had hit me up earlier in the week to come over and set up the computer she had bought. I headed over to handle that for her. She was always trying to keep up with the new technology. She had a Blackberry and I couldn't understand why because she could barely work the remote for her digital cable. But that was grandma; she always wanted to keep her fountain of youth, so to speak. She kept her hair and nails done, and she walked every day for her exercise. She had a slim physique and tried to stay active to prevent life-threatening diseases. I approached her door and knocked.

"Hey sugar," grandma said, excited to see her favorite grandson.

"Hey grandma," I replied as I leaned down and kissed her on the cheek.

"You think you gonna be able to put it together, Mari? The internet guy is supposed to be coming over tomorrow and I want everything set up just right so he can do whatever it is he has to do."

"Yeah, grandma, this is a piece of cake. I just have to connect everything."

"Oh okay. You know I'ma need you to teach me how to work this thing," grandma said.

"I got you grandma. After I'm done teaching you, you gonna be able to write your own software," I said laughing.

"Boy, I don't even know what softwire is," grandma said.

"SOFTWARE, grandma, SOFTWARE," I said laughing.

"Yeah, yeah. You know your cousin pregnant again with another baby?"

"Who? Tamara or Kierra?" I asked.

"Kierra. You know this gonna be her second child," my grandma told me shaking her head.

"She graduating high school this year, right?" I asked while tearing the box open.

"Yeah, she supposed to be graduating this year but I don't know," grandma said.

"Dag, my little cousin slipping. Well, what's up with the baby father? It's the same dude?" I asked.

"Nah, it's a different boy, but he ain't no good either. Your Aunt Jennifer say he locked up just like the other one," grandma said.

"Locked up? How he get locked up?" I asked.

"Round there gang banging and acting a fool. I don't know why she always gets caught up with them hoodlums," grandma said.

"I don't know what it is grandma, but that's what popular nowadays, Your granddaughter seems to like them too," I said.

"My granddaughter who? I know you ain't talking about Sharea," grandma said.

"Yup, your Sha Sha is dating some thug," I said.

"Since when Amari? Do your momma know?" grandma asked.

"Yeah, momma know, but you know Sharea. She really like him so no matter what anybody say she still gonna talk to the boy," I told my grandma as I plugged her keyboard and mouse in to the PC.

"Well, do you know anything about this boy, Amari?"

"Yeah, his name Dante and he went to school with me. He was a grade under me, but even back in high school he was running around in the wrong crowd. Me and his older brother Tamir played on the varsity basketball team together. They cool peoples, but they not for Sharea. They live a very dangerous lifestyle and Sharea got too much going for herself to be involved with them.

"What does he do? He not in school or anything? Does he work anywhere?" grandma asked.

"She said he looking for a job but he trying to become a rapper and he not in school."

"Oh Lord. Well, Amari, ya'll close, so you need to talk some sense into her. I don't see what Kierra and Sharea see in these boys," grandma said.

"I don't know either. I guess they love the bad boys, grandma," I said as I keyed in her administrator information.

"I don't see what's so attractive about a bad boy. A real bad boy will be so bad that he won't be in and out of jail but rather in and out the bank," grandma said.

"They ain't thinking about that, Sharea's more concerned with how good the boy looks than if he gonna be able to provide for her and a baby if they were to take it that far."

"Mari, just keep talking to her and maybe she'll listen to her big brother," grandma said.

"Grandma, I try. I try to tell her but you know how she flips every-thing around. I asked her why she would deal with someone like him, and I told her the dangers that come along with it, but all she did was ask me, 'Well, Amari, what are you doing with your life?' Then she starts going off on me about how I was doing Lauren wrong by cheating on her."

"Well, Amari, I must say she has a point. I been meaning to talk to you about that too. You got to set an example for your sister. If she sees you 'round here becoming a little male whore messing with all these women how you think she gonna feel about that?"

"I understand, grandma, and I changed my ways," I confessed.

"Changed your ways since when? One of your little girlfriends called here the other day looking for you as if you don't have a cell phone," grandma said.

"Today I ended it with all the women I was dealing with. I'm monog-amous now."

"That's good 'cause you got to be careful out here with all these dis-eases running 'round. You don't want to end up like your father."

"Yeah, I definitely don't wanna end up like that loser."

      I wasn't gonna tell her I caught chlamydia because I didn't want her to be worried and upset. I was already disappointed in my-self for hoeing around and there wasn't any need to get anyone else involved. I didn't even tell Tosha. I decided to take it to the grave.

"Well, how is that job coming along, Amari? Have you been thinking about what you want to do long term?"

"The job is cool. I'm still the assistant manager, but I been thinking about opening up a club or lounge or something."

"Okay, okay, yeah, you've been talking about opening up your own club ever since Jay Z opened up the 40/40 club. That sounds good but what have you been doing to make that happen?"

"I been working at the store a lot so I haven't really looked into it yet. I plan on doing some research on it though soon."

"What are you waiting for, Amari? Don't fall into that cycle that me and your momma fell into. When we were your age we got caught up working making that little bit of money and didn't go to school. Ended up having kids and our dreams died right along with the child support that we never got from ya'll fathers. So if this is what you want to do, you need to start making them steps to go' head and do it."

"Yeah, I hear you grandma, but there are so many nightclubs. I got to figure out what's gonna be so different about mine." I grabbed the computer box filled with bubble wrap and ripped plastic and placed it next to the garbage can.

"I gotta bring something new to the game in order to make it, grandma."

"Come with me to the store. I got to play my Pick-It and I want to show you something," grandma said, grabbing her purse.

We walked down to the corner store. As we were walking, my grandmother pointed out certain things to me.

"See that young kid over there dribbling the ball?

"Yeah"

"He told me yesterday that the NBA is his only hope out of

here. See that young girl pushing a baby in a stroller with one hand, and holding another baby in her arm? You see that drunken man over there sitting on the curb? See them boys out here on this corner? You would think since they out here so much the street would be clean."

"Yeah, I see them grandma. What about them, though?" I asked.

"I'ma tell you as soon as we come out of this store."

I said wassup to the fellas that was outside the store. Most of them I went to school with or just knew from being in the area. I went inside to make sure my grandma didn't spend all her money on the Lotto; she was liable to go overboard. As I walked out of the store I came across an all too familiar face. It was a woman begging for some quarters. She claimed she needed it to get on the bus. I gave her a dollar and went on my way. I had been seeing that same lady begging for money for years now.

"Amari, the reason I pointed those things out to you is because you asked me how you could make your club different from all those other clubs that are out there."

"Okay, so you want me to have a club filled with drug dealers from the corner, a drunken man, a homeless woman, young boys who want to play basketball and a bunch of women with multiple babies?" I asked in confusion.

"No, what I'm saying, Amari, is give your people a chance. Change this city, Amari. Change this world. Make your business more than about making money. Help create better situations for everybody. Help them break the cycle."

info@marquisewatson.com

"Break the cycle? I don't get it grandma," I said.

"Look around you; you see the same story. You see people who had dreams and let their dreams vanish; you see young people dying for an opportunity; you see your people dying for society to accept them, Amari," grandma said.

My grandma had a point. She always seemed to have a point. I think back to my days in high school and I remember hearing everyone talk about their big plans and everything they wanted to do. Many wanted to become rappers, singers, authors, comedians, business owners, fashion designers, engineers; the list went on and on. None of those people, including myself, are doing anything of the sort. We are not even in the process of becoming the things we were so passionate about becoming. Some of us made it to college, but ended up dropping out after a year or two.

"You're right, grandma. I guess it is up to me to break the cycle. The ones who were fortunate enough to make it out, never came back to help us out. Maybe I could be the first."

"Yes, Amari, it is. We need some change around here. Take advantage of the resources you have around you, and you will get to where you want to be; I guarantee it."

When we got back, I hooked the speakers up to my grandmother's computer and added the last piece of necessary software (or "softwire" as my grandma would call it). We ate peanut butter and jelly sandwiches before I headed home. Some things taste so much better at grandma's house. I couldn't explain it, but a peanut butter and jelly sandwich was one of them. Grandma stopped me as I headed out the door.

"Now, Amari, remember this; there is going to be a time where doing the wrong thing looks more attractive than doing the right thing. It is then when your manhood will be tested."

"OK grandma. Love you, and see you tomorrow."

"Love you too, and tell your momma I'll call her tonight after the news go off. And be safe out there, Amari."

"OK, I will."

Grandma hugged me and kissed me on my cheek.

I went home and hopped straight on my computer. Through the internet, I researched the local club owners; there weren't too many. After taking down their numbers, the names of their clubs, and their addresses, I called the managers and requested some of their time to present my proposals. I viewed their websites and saw all the things they offered, and more importantly I jotted down the things they didn't offer. After researching for hours, I realized that I had a slim to none chance of getting someone to give me the necessary capital to fund my own club. I decided I would persuade someone to make me a partner. My boys used to stay clowning me for working at Victoria's Secret, but for the past two years I've been assistant manager for one of the best name brand stores in the world; I knew that experience had to increase my chances with club owners. I knew it was a monumental task: I was 22 years old, with no type of degree, no prior club experience, and a vision. But the president of the United States was black so I supposed anything was possible at that point.

The clock struck 12 and La La texted me to let me know she made it home safely. Right then I thought to take her out on a picnic the next day after church. She was a big fan of honey BBQ wings and coleslaw. I figured I'd take her to Branch Brook Park, lay out a couple of blankets, play smooth R&B on my boom box, eat some good food and read her a poem. When we first got together I used to write her little poems and letters all the time, but after a while it all stopped. I knew she would be happy and besides what better way was there for me to tell her I was ready to move in with her? She had been getting on me for a while about moving in with her and I'd been brushing her off. I thought about how she was alone at night and how she must wish she had me in the bed to keep her warm. It was time for me to step up and become the best man I could be for her. I knew I couldn't take our relationship for granted. I grabbed my pen and started to write:

Untitled

It's been 4 years now, going on five and I'm looking forward to the longevity
You are the greatest gift ever found and I love you La La unconditionally
When I look into your eyes, and I stare into your soul
I realize, that what I got is more precious than gold
And I really want you to know that I love you girl
The time spent with you is unlike no other person in this world
So understand, that you still got my heart and nothing has changed
And you complete me like a picture does to a frame

Like furniture does to a new place, like an Icee on a summer day
And baby girl, there is nothing else more 2 say, but oh yea
I'm moving in with you today …

-Ya best friend/boyfriend Amari

After that I took it down and went to bed. I had church in the morning and I wanted to surprise my ma and sister by cooking their favorite breakfast. My momma was an early bird. Church started at 11, so she usually got up to cook breakfast at like 8 in the morning. I had to make sure I beat her to the kitchen. I couldn't go to sleep in complete silence so I put the TV on Sports Center and drifted to sleep.

Chapter Five

The smell of buttermilk pancakes and spicy beef sausage woke my mother and sister. These are two of the most important women in my life so I felt it was only right for me to cater to them as much as I could. In this life we can't take nothing for granted.

"Good morning, son. Thanks for cooking; I definitely didn't feel up to it today," my ma thanked me as she began to cut up her pancakes.

"Yeah, I figured you weren't feeling up to it. What's been going on ma?" I asked while drowning my pancakes in Aunt Jemima's syrup.

I knew something was going on with her job because that's the only thing she ever really stressed over. My ma worked for an insurance company, and the way the economy was going, we never knew how long her job was gonna last.

"They just laid off ten people, Amari, and took away our overtime. I don't know what's gonna happen next."

"It's gonna be aight, ma. Don't stress over it. God gonna handle it."

"I'm so glad your sister got that scholarship, but I promised her I was gonna help her get a car, and now I don't know if I'm gonna be able to."

"Don't even worry about it, ma. Sharea will just have to work a few extra hours at her job and I'll look around for some deals on some cars."

I hated this part of my life. I hated to see my mother stress over anything, especially work. My mother used to be so radiant, but life's challenges seemed to take her glow away. Her short hair framed a face weary from worrying about how to balance the family and the checkbook. She used to keep in shape, but she had recently added several pounds to her small frame. Her weight gain and her work-related stress were probably the reasons she had blood pressure problems.

With a hope she could recover some joy through entrepreneurship, I encouraged my mother to go into business for herself. I was sure my mother would be happier if she took a chance on her own venture, as opposed to withering in a dead-end job, but I knew entrepreneurship would not fix everything. My mother's light, and my mother's joy, seemed to ebb over the years as she wrestled with the financial responsibilities she shouldered alone. When I thought back on the hundred dollar sneakers I begged her for, and the $50 video games I only played for a few months before I forgot they existed, I felt stupid. She always made sure my sister and I had everything, and that we wouldn't feel less than the next person because our fathers weren't in the picture.

My sister's father is still alive, but he doesn't do anything for her. He doesn't spend any time with her, and doesn't even bother to call her. She does have a relationship with her grandparents and speaks with them often. They send her cards and money for her birthday and Christmas. Unfortunately, most of us in the urban community grow up like that. Damn. Where are all the dead beat fathers? How could a man father a child and not know anything about the life he created? How could he not want to spend time with his own child? It was cool, though. We had ma and grandma, and as far as I knew, that's all we ever needed.

"Ay ma, I'ma move in with Lauren," I said as I took the last bite of my sausage.

"Oh you are? You sure you ready for that? You been holding out for some time now."

"Yeah, I think I'm ready, and if it don't work out then I'll be knocking on your door," I said laughing.

"OK son, you know you always welcomed here with your momma."

"Yeah, I know, ma. And don't worry; I'ma still give you some money every month like I do now."

"No, Amari, that's OK. You need to pull your weight over there with Lauren."

"Nah ma, you gonna take my money one way or the other. Either you take the cash or I'll be down at public service paying the bill."

"Oh boy," she said, smiling at her young prince.

"Ma, I think you should look into that babysitting business you always been talking about." Sharea finally decided to join us and co-signed my idea about ma going into business.

"Yeah momma, you should try that," Sharea suggested as she fixed her plate.

"I don't know, ya'll. That's a little too risky right now. I'ma have to wait on that."

"Aight ma, but you been waiting your whole life. There's no better time than right now," I told her before I went in my room to get dressed for church.

She didn't say anything back. She just sat there and finished eating her pancakes. I did my thing making those; I'd become quite a chef. My momma used to always tell me while I was growing up that a woman loves a man that can cook for her sometimes. I used to always watch her and my grandma in the kitchen. I wouldn't say I'm as good as them, but I haven't burnt down any houses either, or apartments in our case. I headed out before ma and Sharea so I could pick up Lauren. Lauren and I made it a habit to go to church together. I still did my dirt, but church kept us grounded and gave us strength to overcome things couples go through. There was a lot to overcome when we first got together.

My best friend CJ died when I was 19. He was hit with two shots in his back, and he never recovered. It was a petty death too: all over some Louis Vuitton shoes. His moms got the shoes for him on his birthday, and one night he got robbed after a party. They say he tried to run, but he shouldn't have. I know the sneakers were worth a lot, but his life was worth a whole lot more than $500.

After my friend's murder, I started to act a little different; I started arguing with Lauren and drinking a lot. I started to lose myself. I think it was then that I started to get pissed off at my hood. Niggas get shot every day, but when it's your main nigga, it sort of puts it in a different perspective.

I started carrying a gun on me. Luckily for me I never got caught with it. Thanks to the counsel of Reverend Wilson, I eventually realized that I was taking the wrong approach. Lauren stuck with me through the whole thing and I love her even more for it. She was supportive and understanding and I believe that church played a big part in that. During that time, if we had an argument or any issue, we took special care to attend church and pray on our situation. Now we were four years deep, and aside from all the times I cheated on Lauren, or the chlamydia I could have given her, things ran very smoothly for us. We had stood the test of time. Some relationships do not make it past 6 months so I was blessed to have my La La. I blew the horn to let her know I was outside. She strutted out, looking beautiful as always.

"Morning, my love," I said in my British voice.

"Good morning deacon," she joked back.

She called me "deacon" because I always went to church in something formal. On that day, I wore a classic black three-button pinstripe suit with a lavender button shirt which was brought out by the black and lavender tonal dot silk tie. My black fedora hat protected my waves from the sun and my feet were lifted off the ground by a comfortable pair of black loafers. She dressed just as formal. I couldn't understand why she wore tummy control hosiery; she really didn't have a tummy to control. She wore a silk white ruffle top and the red heels I had just bought her at Elegance. Her matching bag strained to hold the useless things she kept in it. That was another thing I didn't understand about women; I could carry a wallet and be fine. But Lauren had to have a bag full of stuff I thought she could've just kept home.

"How was the movie last night?" I asked giving her a peck on the lips.

"The movie was good - the little bit that I heard. Them rude people kept talking through the entire movie," Lauren said.

"What movie theater did you go to?" I said laughing.

"It isn't funny, Mari. We went to the one downtown. And on top of the rude people talking, some men were outside fighting when we were leaving," Lauren answered.

"Well, now you know not to go to that theater. That's why when we go I don't take you there," I said.

"Well, Brooke wanted to go there because she's cool with someone that works there and he got us in free," Lauren said.

"Well, in that case, maybe we have to go to that movie theater and make sure we bring Brooke with us every time we go," I said laughing.

"Boy, you stupid."

"I'm serious, the movies cost too much nowadays. $20 just to get in. Then the drinks are like $20 and popcorn running $15. If I want a Kit Kat that's another $10," I said.

"It ain't even that much, Mari," Lauren said while laughing.

"Ay babe, on a more serious note, I'ma need you to talk to Sharea for me."

"What's going on, Amari? What's wrong with Sha?"

"She dating this dude, and I don't really feel too comfortable with that whole situation, but you know she ain't trying to listen to her big brother."

"Sharea is getting older and she's gonna date guys Amari," Lauren said while covering her lips with lip balm.

"No, La La. This boy is into that street life and you know Sharea ain't bred for no dude like that. Sharea is a little geek, I don't even know how she stand being with the dude."

"Why you calling Sha a geek? Sha just focused and got her own style," Lauren said.

"Yeah, I'm proud of her for chasing her dream of becoming a teacher, and she's a good girl, but she not using good judgment with this dude. I mean you got her doing her community service with the kids, and his community service is giving drugs to the kids. Now you tell me what's right with that picture. I don't know, babe. I don't know what make him so special."

"The same things that make you special to me, boo. She probably looking past his flaws and looking at him beyond that thug exterior that you and everybody else see," Lauren said.

"La La, personally I don't care what she sees. I don't have a good feeling about her dating him so just talk to her about making good judgments and putting herself in the best positions in life. I think she will take it better from you because she looks up to you."

"Alright I'll see what I can do," Lauren said with an unsure look on her face.

We arrived at church and went in and got an uplifting word from Reverend Wilson. The message was about stepping out on faith, putting all your trust in God, and not worrying about things so much. I felt like he was speaking to me because I had been worrying about my sister and her situation, my mother and her situation, taking that step and moving in with Lauren and my personal struggle to become an accomplished man. I felt like I had become stagnant and like I had lost my sense of who I was over the years. I was falling into the same trap as my ma, my grandma, my aunts, my uncles, and my older cousins; I was passive, but I became upset when things didn't go the way I wanted them to go. Reverend Wilson was definitely talking to me that day. Church was done and I walked to the front to talk to him.

"Hey Rev. Good message," I said.

"Hey Amari. Thanks, man. Listen, I want to meet with you sometime this week or next week. I have something new I'm starting up and I want you to be a big part of it."

"Okay, Rev, just call me and I'll be there."

I gave a few more hugs and kisses to the elder women in the church who played extra grandmas in my life since day one. There was one thing you were certain to get from church every Sunday: a basket full of kisses and a message to think about. I still intended to have the romantic picnic with Lauren so I told my grandma I was gonna miss Sunday dinner. She smiled and told me she was proud of me. She always knew how to make me feel like everything was gonna be alright.

"Ay babe, we not going to grandma's for dinner; I got something else planned. I'ma take you home so you can change your clothes then I'ma come back and pick you up."

"Where are we going, Mari?" Lauren asked.

"It's a surprise."

"Oooh boy, you're so full of surprises," Lauren said.

"Yeah, I know," I said as we pulled off.

"What do you want me to change into, Amari?"

"Throw on some shorts, a beater, and some sandals: something sporty. Show that rich skin of yours."

"Okay, you got me all excited."

I dropped her off at home and headed back to my house to change clothes. Then I went to the Chicken Wing Shack to get honey BBQ wings and coleslaw. With a poem in my pocket, and a few blankets over my shoulder, I arrived at the park and setup my spot. I had four blankets and a few pillows. It was such a beautiful day. The sun was out and the clouds must have been scared because they were nowhere to be found. The air was refreshing. I knew she was gonna love it. The atmosphere was incredible. I had put the food in a picnic basket my mother kept in the pantry. She never used it; I guess it was a gift or something. I left the basket, the blankets, and the boom box, and went to pick up Lauren. She was sitting on the porch waiting for me.

"Babe, I want you to close your eyes the whole ride there," I said.

"Okay, Mr. Spontaneous."

      The park wasn't far from her house, but she closed her eyes and took a quick cat nap. As she reclined the chair back, and caught some zzz, I couldn't help but stare at her when we stopped at red lights. I loved her so much. I got mad at myself all over again for what I had done to her in the past, but I was determined to make sure she never found out. I committed to being an honorable man, going forward. When we arrived, I opened the car door for her like every gentleman should. I walked her to the romantic picnic site.

"OK babe, you can open up your eyes."

She took a second to gaze at everything and busted a big smile.

"Aww baby, you are so amazing! When did you find time to do all of this?" Lauren asked observing the setup.

"Well, unlike some people, it doesn't take me an hour to get dressed."

She took a peep inside the basket.

"Oh my God; you got my favorite wings!"

"Yeah, but I forgot the dessert. Damn, I knew I was forgetting something."

"Don't worry about that, because you're gonna have me for dessert," Lauren said as she gave me a peck on the lips. She was a classic example of, "lady in the streets, freak in the sheets." My baby could get down in the bedroom, but no one would know that from how she carries herself publicly.

"God's greatest dessert," I said as I smiled and turned the boom box up a little.

We danced with one another for what felt like hours. I held her close to my body as our hips swayed to the rhythm of the songs. Our eyes met like words on a Scrabble board and our souls meshed like a weave on a hood rat. We finally got to the food and enjoyed our wings and Cole slaw.

"Ay baby, I got another surprise for you," I said reaching into my pocket to pull out the poem.

"Wow another surprise? What is it this time, baby?"

I gave her the poem and she shed a tear. I always liked tears of joy; they reassured me that I was doing something right. I held her in my arms for a few seconds and looked up to the sky to thank God for this beautiful situation.

"Baby, are you moving in for real?"

"Yes, babe. Tonight, if you don't mind."

"Oh my GOD, baby!!! I'm so happy," Lauren responded while giving me a hug.

"I'm glad you are; that's my aim, babe."

We lay on the blankets and stared into the sky. I had so many thoughts jogging around my mind. The most important ones concerned my newfound ambition to take this club thing serious. I had what I felt like were good qualities to offer a club owner. My grandma was right; it was time for me to do something and not only dream of becoming what I wanted to be. I needed to take proactive steps towards becoming what I wanted to be.

"La La, I had a talk with grandma the other day and she was getting on me about what I wanted to do long term, as far as life and my career and everything. I decided I'ma take this club thing seriously."

"OK, so you finally gon' go hard with the club idea?" Lauren asked, rolling over to lay her head on my chest.

"Yeah, I was walking with grandma to the store, and she pointed out how many of us have dreams, but we may not see the avenue for it or have the resources to attain it. I was thinking like I could create that opportunity for some of those individuals by opening up my own club."

"So how you plan on doing that?"

"Well, you know a bank isn't gonna give me a loan. I was thinking of trying to negotiate some type of partnership deal. I don't know, babe, but I gotta do something. I ain't trying to be working at Victoria's Secret my whole life. I wanna do my own thing."

"I hear you, babe, and you will. What you been thinking about doing at the club, though?"

"I was thinking of having a comedy night, an open mic night for local rappers, a poetry night, dance competitions, and fashion shows, which will let up and coming designers show off their designs. And for those that want to start a lingerie line, I could give them a few pointers."

"I like that. That'll give me a chance to display my accessory line when I get the pieces made," Lauren said.

"Yeah, exactly. This way you can get a response from people you don't know and generate some interest for your line."

"Yeah, that's great, babe," she said wincing.

"What's wrong babe, you okay?"

She sat up with a look of pain on her face. "Yeah, I'm okay. I just got a sharp pain," she answered holding her stomach.

"You want me to take you to the hospital?"

"Nah, it's OK. Let's just go home and lie down."

I grabbed the blankets and pillows, put the boom box inside the picnic basket, and headed to the car. To make her more comfortable, I positioned the pillow in her seat so she could lie down and rest on the drive back to my house. My lil' momma wasn't feeling too good, so I wanted to get her home quickly. I grabbed some underclothes, a couple of T-shirts, my work uniform and some kicks and headed back to my new home.

Chapter Six

It was Monday and almost time to get rid of the past completely. Nurse Ellen said the clinic opened up at 9:00 am so I made sure to be there at 8:45. Lauren was still sick; she even called out from work. She was a preschool teacher, and she loved those kids to death, so I knew something must've been wrong for her to call out.

I approached the treatment center and was surprised to see so many people there. There had to be at least five other people waiting. I didn't know if they were getting treated, or if they were getting tested, but I doubted anyone would wake up that early just to get tested. Like me, they were probably getting treated, but that thought didn't lessen my embarrassment.

When my turn came, I made the unfortunate discovery that the cure was in liquid form. I was hoping for a pill, or a shot, but instead they gave me a liquid antibiotic and it tasted horrible. It was the nasty aftertaste left by my nights of scandalous fun with women I barely knew. I had risked my health and my relationships with Lauren, my mother, my grandma, and my sister. I drank the cup and thanked the Lord for saving me from what could have been an even worse disease. The nurse had a few words for me before I rushed out of that horrid place.

"Amari, the infection should clear up within seven to fourteen days. Please refrain from sex during this time so that you do not risk transmitting the disease to your partner."

"Okay, thanks," I said, eager to leave and put it all behind me.

"Another thing, Amari, here are some condoms; please use them. You were very fortunate not to have caught a more serious STD," she said giving me the bag of condoms.

I took them and left out. It was still early and I had a craving for my grandma's cheese eggs, sausage and grits. I called her and asked if she would mind making me some. As always she said, "They'll be ready by the time you get here."

I was spoiled with the simple things in life, I didn't have the dream car, or the dream home, or a lot of money, but I had a lot of love. That's most important, but, I had dreams of a better life for my family. Many families are ripped apart by the hood, and I was determined to make sure mine wasn't one of them. My family was all I had: I was nothing without it. Even though there weren't many of us outside of my immediate family - just a few cousins, aunts and uncles - we were extremely close.

I arrived at my grandmas and the smell hit me from the porch. It brought me back to the days when she used to take me to school in the morning: she always made sure my sister and I had a hot meal to start the day. She didn't believe in Frosted Flakes or Oatmeal, she was old school with it. It was sausage, grits, eggs, buttermilk pancakes: something that required actual time to make.

"Good morning grandma. How you feeling?"

"I'm alive, so I can't complain, sugar."

"You know I decided to move in with Lauren?"

"Oh you did, huh? Well, what caused this sudden change of heart?"

"Our talk we had the other day. I realized that I have to take control of my life a little more and Lauren had been asking me for some time now to move in with her and I love her so I don't see why not," I answered.

"You know what I think? I think you're becoming a man, Amari," grandma said with a smile on her face as she sipped on her coffee.

"I guess so grandma, thanks to you," I said.

While we watched The View, I sat at the kitchen table eating what I called a gourmet meal. I called the wifey to check up on her and make sure she wasn't dead or nothing. She let me know that she was feeling much better and that she was cleaning up the place. I had set an appointment to meet the manager at Club Luxury, one of the local clubs, to see if I could possibly do business with him. I didn't have to be back to work until Wednesday so I decided to make the best of my free time. I wrote down my ideas and outlined what I could bring to the table as a partner. I finished my plate, placed it in the sink and changed into the suit I kept in the closet in my grandma's spare room. I spent a lot of time with my grandma so I made sure to have some clothes at her place for the nights I slept over.

"Grandma, I'ma check up on you later. I have an appointment to talk to the manager of Club Luxury," I said.

"OK, Mari. Good luck and let me know how it turns out."

After I gave her a hug and kiss goodbye, I drove towards a potential new future for me and my family. I knew that if I was to land this position it could change everything. I wanted to take the stress off my momma. Her job was her main cause of stress, but in addition to that she suffered from high blood pressure. I wanted to give her the chance to do what she always dreamed: open her babysitting service. She had me at an early age and she understood the struggles of young girls my age. She wanted to give them a safe place to drop their kids off without breaking their pockets. My mom wasn't into flashy things. She didn't care about getting rich. She just wanted to be comfortable. That was just about everybody in the hood. They weren't trying to get rich; they just wanted to be able to pay bills on time and maybe take a little vacation. I'm a little different, though. I must've gotten the drive to be rich from my sperm donor father because Lord knows I want it all. I thought about my little sister, my heart, I wanted to get her a nice car and allow her to focus on her schoolwork while I took care of her bills. My grandma always talked about taking a vacation out of the country. I wanted to give her that so badly. I thought about Lauren, the woman I considered to be my future wife and mother of my kids. We were living on the first floor of a two family house now, but I wanted to have a big house for our future family. I wanna provide for her in a way no man ever provided for my mother. My desires were good, so I believed God would make a way for me to get to where I wanted to be.

I arrived at Club Luxury and was very impressed by the feng shui. Although it was my first time at the club, a few of my coworkers talked about the parties they had here. I used to joke about co-workers whose tales of weekend drunkenness would conclude with the sentence "and I threw up on everything!" The place was so high energy, I thought to myself as I walked through the lobby and was greeted by a receptionist.

"Good afternoon, sir. Can I help you?"

"Good afternoon. I have an appointment to meet Mr. Rodriguez," I said.

"And what is your name, sir?"

"Amari Crews."

She began to look at the club's scheduler.

"Okay, yes, I see you have an appointment. Give me a second; I will go and get him."

As I stood and waited my hands began to sweat, my mouth became desert dry, and suddenly my heart was racing as if I had just run a marathon. Moments later there he was: I was in awe. You know the saying "you look like a million bucks?" Well, this man looked like a BILLION bucks. His suit had the initials RDR on them and unlike normal suits, his seemed to be shining. It wasn't like Diddy and Mase in the 90's but he had a certain glow. Nothing was dull about him, he was clean cut: shoes shined, watch shined. I was blinded.

"Good afternoon, Mr. Crews. How are you?"

I shook his hand. "Good afternoon, Mr. Rodriguez."

"OK, Mr. Crews, on the phone you told me you had some ideas. Tell me more about these ideas. I'm always looking for new ways to improve my club."

"Well, being from where I'm from, I see a lot of young people misusing the time that they have. That misuse of time causes them to get into negative situations and I believe I have a solution to help change some of those negative situations into opportunities. I was thinking Club Luxury could have an open mic night every Tuesday and a comedy night on, let's say, Wednesday. We could host fashion shows for up and coming designers and models. We could have some aspiring DJs work a few Saturday night parties, and hold concerts here for underground rappers and singers."

"Those are good ideas but that sounds like a lot of work and a lot of time," Mr. Rodriguez said.

"Yes, and I'm willing to put in the time and work to make it happen. I think this would be great for the community."

"I agree; it definitely would be great for the community. How old are you Mr. Crews?"

"I'm 22, sir," I answered.

"Just 22? You look much older," Mr. Rodriguez added. "Well, do you have any experience working at a club?"

"No, but I've been working at Victoria's Secret since my junior year in high school and I have developed other skills that I believe will help me succeed in the proposed partnership."

"Have you graduated college, Mr. Crews?" he asked.

"No, I have never been to college, but I have been assistant manager for my store for the past two years."

"Mr. Crews, I like your ambition. It takes a lot of courage to walk in here and I can tell you're passionate. I'm sorry to say that I don't have the time to watch over anyone, or teach an apprentice. The truth is, with no prior experience or education, I'm afraid this position is more demanding than you're prepared for," he said.

"I understand, sir, but I have a great work ethic. I'll do anything to make sure business is done well," I said, pleading with him for an opportunity.

He adjusted his tie, sat up in his fancy chair and said, "Amari, I am going to tell you this because I get a good vibe from you. This is what I think you should do. I think you should go to school and develop a sound business foundation. In school you will learn the necessary tools that you are going to need to be successful in this business. Do lots of reading. While you're eating at a restaurant, or while you are attending social gatherings, try networking with as many people as possible. This way you can be exposed to even more knowledge."

"OK, thank you. Thank you so much for your time, Mr. Rodriguez."

"No problem. I'm glad I can be of some help to you, Amari," Mr. Rodriguez said as we shook hands.

As I walked out of the club I felt horrible. My ma told me to go to school and get my education. I was so happy to graduate high school, and get away from the boring life of classes, that I just stuck with my job. Well, there was nothing I could do, but dust myself off and do what I had to do. Although I was dejected, I knew Lauren was home waiting for me. She was my comfort and always knew how to brighten my day.

I walked in the door to a clean home and food on the stove. I could definitely get used to this. We sat in the living room and began to eat.

"Hey baby, how did everything go at the club?" Lauren asked.

"Not the way I wanted it to," I said with a long face.

"Well don't sweat it; the next club owner will see the vision. Come here," Lauren said.

She was so supportive and optimistic about everything and I needed that. We sat on the couch and looked at some of the designs she had drawn for her accessory line. So far she only had a few handbags and belts. Her vision was to provide simple and classy accessories for both women and men. The name of the line, Exquisite, was fitting. As it began to go into the wee hours of the night, I received a call from a good friend of mine, Shawn.

"Ay, Mari, your sister down here in the crib bugging," he said.

"What you mean she down there bugging? Where you at?"

"We over here on Wilcox. My little cousin had a Wii tournament so a bunch of us over here. But she sitting over here with some dude smoking kush and drinking E&J and I know that's not her. That's why I'm calling you up now."

"Thanks man, I appreciate it. What's the address? I'm on my way over there to get her right now," I said pissed off.

"55 Wilcox, don't come over here busting, my nigga," he said jokingly.

"Nah, not even. I'm always calculated, never crazy."

I yanked my shirt off the dresser and slammed the drawer as I put my socks on.

"Baby, what's the matter? Who was that?" Lauren asked wondering why I appeared so angry.

"That was my friend. Sharea done lost her fucking mind," I said, still angry.

"What happened? What Sha do, Mari?"

"She's over there getting drunk and smoking weed with her boyfriend and a bunch of other people."

"So what are you about to do, Mari?"

"What you think I'm about to do? I'm about to go yank her ass out of there and take her home."

"Wait, Amari, let me go with you before you do something stupid," Lauren said.

We got in the car and sped over to Wilcox.

"I can't believe this girl. She don't even drink apple cider, but now she want to get drunk off of E&J," I spoke out loud as my foot weighed heavy on the pedal.

"Baby, calm down and slow down. When we get there just let me do all the talking, okay, because once you start yelling and going off she just gonna shut down and not even listen to you."

We arrived and I attempted to get out of the car.

"Amari, stay in the car. I'ma go get her," Lauren insisted.

After about five minutes Lauren walked outside with Sharea.

"Sharea, what the hell is wrong with you?" I yelled as they got in the car.

"Amari be quiet and just drive," Lauren said trying to make sure the situation didn't get out of hand.

I was heated; Sharea seemed out of it and she smelled like a marijuana cloud. I was so disappointed in her. It's one thing when you have a history of drinking and smoking, but she wasn't like that, and I knew it was that dude talking her into doing these things which were so uncharacteristic of her. I took her home and we all went inside. I had to get more clothes from my old room and Lauren wanted to show Sharea some things on the internet about the danger she was putting herself in.

EFFECTS OF SMOKING MARIJUANA

1. Long term marijuana use can lead to ADDICTION. This will affect social functioning in the context of school, family, work, etc. According to some studies, abusers who try to quit experience irritability, sleeplessness, decreased appetite, anxiety, and drug craving.

2. Increased rates of depression, schizophrenia, suicidal ideation, and anxiety.

3. After the first hour of smoking marijuana your chance of heart attack increases four times as it raises your blood pressure and reduces oxygen carrying capacity in the blood.

4. IT IS MORE LIKELY TO GIVE YOU CANCER THAN CIGARETTES!

After she advised Sharea of marijuana's effects, Lauren shared some information on the long term effects of drinking alcohol. It is well documented that the short term effects include vomiting and impaired ability, but it doesn't end there.

EFFECTS OF DRINKING ALCOHOL

1. Severe anxiety, tremors, hallucinations, and convulsions.

Permanent damage to vital organs such as the liver and brain and potentially, lessening the years of your life.

Visit: www.marquisewatson.com

"So Sharea do you understand now why it wasn't such a good choice to do what you were doing?" Lauren asked.

"Yeah, I understand, but I didn't know it was that serious," Sharea responded.

"Did your boyfriend make you do these things Sharea?" Lauren put her arms around Sharea's shoulders to embrace her.

"No, but he asked me to try it and I didn't want to embarrass him in front of his friends because they were all there having a good time."

"Sharea, if Dante can't respect the fact that you're not into those activities then maybe you need to reevaluate your relationship with him."

"You're right. I know Amari is so upset with me; I hate when he gets mad at me," Sharea said as she shed a tear.

"It's okay, girl. We all make mistakes, and don't worry about your brother; I'll handle him." Lauren comforted Sharea with a hug and wiped her face.

I walked in and saw them showing each other love. I was still furious, but I didn't want to end the night with my sister like that so I went over and gave her a hug. I thought Lauren's method of getting to Sharea worked a little bit. I was happy that they had that type of relationship. In Lauren, Sharea had an older sister who could advise her when big brother didn't have the tools (or the feminine finesse) to do so.

"Sharea, we're about to leave. Your clothes stink: you need to wash them ASAP before mommy smells them and you need to take a shower and brush your teeth," I said as calmly as possible.

I left the house and went on home. The bed looked extra good to me when I got there. Lauren and I jumped in it and let the TV do the rest.

Chapter Seven

Days went by. I worked my hours for Victoria's Secret, but I continued hitting up other clubs in hopes of establishing business relationships. No luck so it was back to the pearberry. It was becoming more and more stressful working at my job. Those 8 hour days I spent at work I could have spent working on making things pop off, but no, I continued to rearrange the push-ups. I kept hearing the same things: no college education and no experience equal no business. I thought I had racked up plenty of business experience as the assistant manager for Victoria's Secret. Maybe my would-be partners didn't believe in me at that moment, but I took advantage of my assistant manager position to meet people in stores and make connections. Something had to pop. I was getting stressed, and the pressure was on. My momma had lost a lot in her 401k due to the financial market debacle. That was a major concern because she had often dipped into her 401K to pay her bills. My sister had just gotten laid off from her job because the company had gone out of business. She had been a customer service associate for Circuit City. The job market was getting worse depending on what field you were in. Lauren had some security with her job but she struggled to save the capital needed to produce her accessory line. Then there was me, the man of the family, the man that was supposed to make everything better. Being assistant manager at Victoria's Secret wasn't as cool as it once was. It paid the bills, but it wasn't enough. But I shouldn't have complained; I was lucky to have a job. Still, I definitely wasn't content.

I needed some words of wisdom so I headed to my church to talk to my pastor. He was a down to earth dude, and we had a good friendship. He was sort of that father figure I needed. He helped me get through losing my best friend, and I knew he would put things in the right perspective for me.

"Hey Rev, you got a minute?" I asked, knocking on the door to his office.

"Of course, Amari. Come have a seat. What's up?"

"It's so much going on right now. I moved in with Lauren, my sister got this boy all in her head, and I been chasing a dream that don't seem to be coming to a reality."

He offered me a peppermint from the candy dish. "Well, let's take it one thing at a time. How has it been living with Lauren?"

"It's been interesting. I definitely see another part of her, but it's cool."

"How long has it been now, about what, four, five years you two been together?"

"Yeah, it'll be five years in a couple months." I cracked a smile. "It's been the best years of my life."

"That's a good long time. So don't you think you two should be getting married?"

"I been thinking about marrying her lately. I mean, she's a beautiful person all around. She's supportive, she reminds me of my mom so much, and she has a great relationship with the family."

"OK, well, that's definitely something you should put a lot of thought into. If you truly believe that she's the one you want to spend the rest of your life with then pray on it and do what you have to do. Technically speaking, you two should be married already since you're shacking up."

"Yeah, you right. I'm definitely gonna pray on it. I feel so blessed to have her as one of the women in my life. I just wanna make sure I have things perfect first," I said.

"Amari, nothing is ever perfect, and you shouldn't wait for perfection to come because it never will," Reverend Wilson said, as his secretary came in to give him some papers.

"You're right, Rev."

"Speaking of the women in your life, what's this about Sharea?"

"She's at that age. She's 18 and her nose is busted wide open over this boy," I said shaking my head.

"Well, Amari, weren't you with Lauren at her age? I remember your nose being extremely wide, so what's the problem?"

"The problem is he's been a negative influence on her and she's blinded by this so-called love. You know Sharea; she's a good girl."

"Amari, let me tell you something, as much as you might want to protect her from making mistakes, you have to let her live and learn."

"I guess you right, Rev. I guess you right."

"Now what's this dream you talking about?" Rev asked.

"I'm trying to own my own club," I said.

"A club?" He asked with a perplexed look on his face.

I laughed a little and let him know the deal: "Nah, not like a strip club or anything."

"Well, what type of club are you talking about?"

"A club that serves as a creative outlet: not just a place to embark on the worldly pleasures."

"Okay, so how have you been going about it?"

"I mean, I'm not qualified for a business loan, so I been doing a lot of reading and meeting with different club owners seeing if I can add my touch to their establishment in some type of way."

"How are they responding to your proposal?"

"I been getting no love. Every last one of them rejected me."

Reverend Wilson began feeding the fish in his fish tank. "What are you bringing to the table that's going to make these already established businessmen even remotely interested?"

"Innovative ideas. When you think of most of the nightclubs around here they're all so similar to one another."

"So how do you plan to make your nightclub different from the rest?"

"I want to create a more effective buzz and interest around whichever nightclub I become affiliated with. Nowadays people think of nightclubs as a setting to just dance and meet people, have a few drinks, and listen to great music."

He nodded his head to agree.

"Well, let's keep that thought, but also add in opportunity," I said.

"Okay, I'm hearing you, but what exactly do you mean by opportunity?"

"I'm sure you look around and you see so many talented young people with limited platforms to display their talent. I just want to provide that place where we could have a good time while also expressing ourselves. I want to create a platform where we can show the world our passions and our skills and gain some fulfillment."

"Okay, I like what I'm hearing, but tell me, what are some of your suggestions?"

"For example, my sister's boyfriend, he wants to become a rapper, well what greater place to show off your rap ability than a club filled with people who listen to that kind of music?"

"I agree," he said.

"So I was thinking of having open mic night for rappers and singers, spoken word night for poets, dance competitions, fashion shows in which up and coming designers can show off their artistry and models can also show off their skills. There's so much more to do to generate extra revenue besides what's already being done," I said.

"Amari, I think you have something going here," he told me as our discussion was interrupted by a call. "Hold on Amari, let me take this."

The fact that he thought my ideas were good gave me that extra vote of confidence. While he talked business on the phone I sat there looking around his office. I never really looked at them before when I visited his office but this time I noticed all of his plaques and certificates. He was so accomplished, and I wanted to know what that felt like.

He got off the phone. "Yes, sorry about that but I definitely think you have some good ideas to work with."

"Yeah, but I need someone that's going to believe in me, someone who sees the vision and cares about the community. I mean, people watch the news and always want to talk bad about the hood environment but never want to do anything to improve the environment. So I look at myself in the mirror and ask myself, why not me?"

"Well, Amari, a very good friend of mine just opened up a club about a month ago and he has that same philanthropic spir —-."

"Oh for real? You think you can talk him into giving me a chance?" I was so excited I didn't even let him finish.

"I can't promise you anything, Amari. You will have to work hard for this. I will give him a call though and tell him he should connect with you and hear your ideas. The rest is on you," he said.

"Yes! Thanks so much, Rev. I really appreciate it. I just need that chance." In the back of my mind I knew I had this in the bag. This was too great. I'll probably get a call tomorrow, meet with him the same day, and just like that, I'll be in business.

"You're welcome, but remember, he's my friend, but I don't help him run his business, so don't think it's going to be an automatic you're in there type thing," he said, trying to put it in perspective for me. It didn't work.

We chatted for another hour or so about sports, about life, and about the state of the economy. As I was leaving the office he had some parting words for me.

"Amari, I know you're young, and at this age life is hitting you hard and fast, and you're not used to it yet, but I must tell you this: life is difficult, as I'm sure you know, but once you understand it, I mean truly understand it, and accept it, the fact that it is difficult won't even matter."

I thought about what he said, gave him a hug, and left. My mood was much better, mainly because I knew I had some great ideas. Sooner or later somebody would give me a chance. I headed to the mall to make a quick stop in the jewelry store to buy Lauren something simple and special. Walking past the food court I ran into Tosha.

"Ay Tosha, wassup?" I attempted to hug her.

She extended her hand out to stop me from touching her. "Now you wanna show me some love, not when I been texting you and you ain't been responding back to me." She said with a disgusted look on her face.

"Oh nah, I had to change my number, wassup though?" I went in for another hug to try to make sure she knew it wasn't a diss.

"Uh-huh," she said in a sarcastic tone. "What was that message about, Amari?"

I played dumb like I didn't know what she was talking about. "What message are you talking about?"

"Amari, you know what I'm talking about. You sent me a message basically saying you ain't wanna kick it with me no more. I thought we had a good connection."

"Oh nah, it ain't even like that. I just been going through some things and I need to slow down and put my life in perspective."

"Yeah, yeah, tell me anything," Tosha said as we walked over to Mrs. Fields.

"I put in a good word to my manager for you too. I ain't forget about you." I said before I told the cashier to bag me up two sugar cookies.

"Yeah, I actually just left your job. Your manager said he was gonna give me a call and let me know whether or not they were going to hire me."

"Oh okay, you gonna most likely get hired unless something happen where they—," my phone disrupted my train of thought as I heard my mother's ring tone. I grabbed my Blackberry off the holster.

"Hey ma," I answered.

"AMARI! AMARI! SHAREA'S BEEN SHOT," my mother screamed through the phone.

Shocked and scared to death, I asked, "SHE'S BEEN WHAT? WHAT YOU MEAN? IS SHE OK?"

"She's not responding right now. She's at the hospital and they are working on her now."

"OK, what hospital? What hospital?" I said, throwing the Mrs. Fields bag into the trash can.

"St. Jeffries," she replied through her tears.

"OK, I'm on my way," I said, rushing towards the mall exit.

"Amari, what's wrong? Where are you going?" Tosha yelled out to me.

Now running, I yelled back, "I'll tell you later." Whether she heard me or not was a different story.

I sped to St. Jeffries, swerving in and out of lanes hoping the cops wouldn't see me. Tears raced down my face, and my heart pounded as if it was trying to break from my chest. My stomach cramped up and my muscles tightened with shock. So much was going through my head: I felt as if I had just been shot (as if I knew how that felt). I arrived at the hospital and was shocked again. As I walked through the sliding doors, I was surprised to see Lauren sitting in a wheelchair while a nurse attempted to roll her away.

"Baby, what are you doing here? What's wrong?"

"Hey baby, I'm not feeling good at all. I been throwing up and my chest is hurting," she said placing her hands over her chest. I left you a message. Did you get it?"

"No, Sha has been shot. That's why I'm here," I said as I scanned the emergency room to see if I could spot my mother.

"She's been shot? Who, what, how, Amari?"

"I don't know, but I see my mother, and I'm about to go see what's going on. I'ma check on you in a little bit," I said.

Damn, shit, shit, shit. This was the worst fucking day of my life. I saw my mom and my grandma wailing. Sharea must have been with her friend at the time because her best friend Cecily was crying next to them.

"Ma, what happened? What are they saying about Sharea?"

"Amari, I don't know. She's been shot in the head, and they don't know if she's going to make it. They in there working on her now. All the doctor could say was it's not looking good but they're gonna try their best," my ma cried out grabbing the hand of my grandma.

I tried to hold it in, but I couldn't help but cry. I couldn't believe what was happening. My little sister was dying at the age of 18.

"Well, Cecily, were you there? I mean, what happened?" I asked.

"We were chilling at Jahad's house."

"Who the hell is Jahad?" I said raising my voice at her friend as if she was the shooter.

"Jahad is Dante's cousin. We were at his house and Dante was showing off his new gun. Sha told him to chill; we both told him to chill and stop swinging that thing around but he wouldn't stop playing. He just wouldn't stop. He kept tryna act out stupid gangster movies. Then his cousin Jahad grabbed the gun and started playing around and then out of nowhere the gun went off. He claimed he didn't know it was loaded but he shot her right in the head by mistake."

"Well, where did they go when all of this happened?" I asked in a slightly calmer tone than before.

"They got scared and ran off when I called the ambulance," Cecily said, as more tears poured down her pale face.

I was furious, but all I could do was pray. I sat there with my eyes closed, tears drenching my face. I was angry as a bull, but I put my faith in God to rescue my sister and heal Lauren. I thought about the time Sharea almost drowned in the hotel pool at one of our family reunions years ago. I had to be around thirteen, and she was about nine or so. I was so busy trying to talk to this girl that I didn't even notice Sharea was drowning. One of our older cousins had to come to her rescue. I felt bad then that I wasn't there to protect her and I felt even worse as we waited in the hospital.

After I almost put a dent in the floor from pacing for what seemed like hours, my sister's doctor came out to tell us the news. "We took the bullet out, but she has suffered bilateral damage to her reticular formation of the hindbrain."

"What does that mean doctor?" I asked hoping to get some plain talk in return.

"She has been put in a medically induced coma. We're going to have to monitor her day to day," he said.

"Oh God," my mother shouted out disappointed about the news.

"Doctor, can you explain exactly what happened?" I asked trying to figure out what was going on.

"The shot to her head caused damage to some of her brain tissues, which causes swelling. If it swells too much it could squeeze off her blood supply and she could die."

My grandma jumped in and asked the doctor, "Well, what are her chances?"

"If the swelling does not increase, she has an excellent chance of recovery. We will closely monitor the situation and do the best we can." The doctor said, as he attempted to give us hope.

"Well, can we go see her?" I asked.

"Sure you can."

"Thanks Doc. Thanks a lot," I said wiping a tear from my face.

I wasn't happy she was in a coma, but the news could've been much worse than that. The doctor could have came out and said she passed away. I thanked the Lord as my mother, my grandma, Cecily and I went inside to see her. I couldn't bear to see her like that for too long so I gave her a kiss on the cheek and went to see what was going on with Lauren. A nurse directed me to Lauren's room.

"La La, how are you feeling?"

"I'm fine. How is Sharea? Is she okay?"

"She's in a coma so we just have to be positive," I said.

"Amari, what happened?" she asked still in shock.

"Babe, it's a long story. First tell me what is going on with you. Has the doctor been in here to tell you anything?"

"No, they ran a few tests and hooked me up to this I.V. to give me some fluids and control the nausea."

I was hoping Lauren had a minor stomach virus or something like that. Her doctor came in with unexpected news.

"Lauren, after running your tests…," the doctor said.

"How bad is it doc?" I asked.

"Well, it's not bad at all, Lauren you are two weeks pregnant," the doctor said as my mouth dropped open.

"She's what?" I asked, hoping that the answer would somehow be different.

"She's two weeks pregnant, congratulations." The doctor smiled while Lauren and I were speechless.

I was in a daze as the doctor asked Lauren a series of questions and advised her to see her gynecologist right away so that she could begin prenatal care.

I dropped my head, closed my eyes, and sat in silence. I couldn't believe my ears. First my sister gets shot in the head, and now Lauren is pregnant. I couldn't believe the day I was having.

The doctor left us and Lauren had a puzzled look on her face. After a few minutes went by, I decided to crack the silence, "Well, La La, what you wanna do?"

"I don't know, Mari. I don't know. What do you want to do?"

"It's not up to me," I said.

"Yes it is. You have a say in this too, Amari,"

"It's on you, Lauren. I mean, I would hate for you to go through that whole abortion process but at the same time, are we ready?"

"Our place isn't big enough. We really not accomplished the way we want to be. I don't know boo," Lauren said.

"Well, I'ma let you know this: I'm here, babe, and if you decide to have this baby I ain't gonna leave you like my father did me. I'ma just have to step up to the plate."

"I know, babe. I know," Lauren said lying back down in the hospital bed.

I went outside to think and get a breath of fresh air. I talked to myself a lot; some might call it crazy but I think it's crazy if you don't talk to yourself sometimes. All I could think of was life and its difficulties. I was faced with yet another challenge, another hurdle to jump over. Only 22 and I haven't accomplished anything yet as a man. Who was I to have a baby? Who was I to be responsible for the life of another human being? Catching a STD due to immature and ignorant actions, choosing a 12 dollar an hour job over broadening my education in college, and carrying a cavalier attitude towards life and growth for most of my life, all seemed to disqualify me from deserving the blessing of a child. The only positive thing I had done was keep myself out of the prison system and that wasn't much of an accomplishment.

Sure, I had what most might consider a hard work ethic because of my job, and I had the right attitude as far as making sure to be in my child's life, but like staying out of the prison system, those were bare minimums. How could I successfully raise a child when I myself had yet to be raised? Sure, I knew how to go to a grocery store and buy milk and pampers, and yes, I had the ability to show my child love, but was that enough? What about the psychological things that play a big part in raising children? Should I beat my kid if he or she was to misbehave? How could I ensure my kids didn't repeat my mistakes? What changes did I have to make to become a great parent? I didn't know the answers to those questions. I still lived in the hood, and I loved my hood, but I wasn't convinced it was the ideal place to raise a child. There is violence everywhere, but the hood has the worst kind. It's heartbreaking to see your mother crying at night because she don't know how she gonna feed you. So many evils present themselves in this environment. My mind raced, but I didn't have a clue as of what to do. Still, over the years I had developed a relationship with God and I knew one way or another He would guide me in the right direction.

I thought about Lauren. Lauren never really had a mother. Her mother gave birth to her when she was 18 and resorted to crack after she was born. Her father was a dead-beat. He was young and he refused to shoulder his responsibilities. Her grandmother raised her and was the only real comforting loving figure in her life growing up. Unfortunately she lost her grandma to breast cancer two years ago. I wondered how she would be as a mother. How would she respond to the new adversity and responsibility she would face if she decided to have this child? I walked back into the room and asked, "So what you think La La? Do you want to keep it?"

"I don't know if I am. I got to think about it. Let's give it some time. A lot is going on right now," Lauren said.

I gasped, "Yeah, you right."

We stayed at the hospital for another hour and then Lauren

and I went home. The next few days were stressful; my sister was still in her coma, and we spent many hours at the hospital waiting and praying that Sharea would somehow wake up. Lauren was feeling better, but she still wrestled with whether she wanted to keep the baby. I did everything I could to make her feel as good as possible. I cooked her food (we didn't eat out any more), and I made sure she had nice cold drinks. I didn't want her eating fast food or anything that would be detrimental to the baby. I knew every little thing was important because anything that affected her, affected our baby. She loved the extra attention. I was taking my newfound responsibility head on like a man. Whether my girl ultimately decided to have an abortion, I had to prepare for the possibility of a baby and I had to make sure my girl was comfortable during her pregnancy. If she gave birth to our seed, I would be responsible for taking care of the family. I didn't want her to work anymore, but I had yet to begin an entre-preneurial venture to really provide for her. Reverend Wilson's friend had yet to call me. When I wasn't working at Victoria's Secret, I vis-ited my sister and took care of my Lauren. I looked at work with a whole new perspective. Before, when I was stressed, I'd go shopping and buy myself a pair of sneakers and a couple of T-shirts or some-thing. Shopping always eased my spirit, but those days were done; I watched every cent that passed into our home.

Chapter Eight

On Tuesday morning I cooked Lauren some breakfast before she headed off to work. Then, I headed out to the court to play ball with the fellas. Basketball was a form of therapy for me. There was nothing like being out on the court, all sweaty, competing against a bunch of men who hated to lose. It was priceless and there was something about the game that gets your mind off of everything. After we lost the tough fought game, I decided to go check on my grandma. I also needed to talk to grandma about this whole baby situation and get her opinion on how we were to move forward. Grandma always had something wise to say. I guess it came with her age, and I always felt better after every conversation. As I pulled up I saw her sitting on the porch, in her chair, reading the newspaper. It was a beautiful day, around 75 degrees, with a pleasant breeze.

"Hey grandma. Out here enjoying the weather, huh?" I said bending down to give her a hug and kiss on the cheek.

"Yeah, figure I come out here and get a little fresh air. Have you been to the hospital to check on Sharea today?" grandma asked as she put the newspaper down by her side.

"Nah, I didn't get over there yet. I'ma go over there after I leave here."

"I just came back from seeing her. I still can't believe it," grandma said.

"Yeah, but Sha strong. She gon' get through this," I said holding on to the hope the doctor gave us.

"Yeah, I have been praying on it. How is Lauren feeling?"

"She's doing a little better; she has her days."

I paused and took a deep breath as I let it out, "Grandma, Lauren is pregnant."

"SHE'S PREGNANT? Get outta here! When did you find this out, Amari?" grandma asked, stunned by the news.

"The same day Sha got shot. Lauren was throwing up, and was having chest pains, so the doctor ran tests and saw she was two weeks pregnant."

"Oh my Lord. How many times have I told you to wear your raincoat when you fooling around? I been telling you that since you were in high school. What are you going to do, Amari?"

"I really don't know, grandma. I told Lauren it was up to her."

"Do you think you're ready for a child, Amari? You're only 22 years old."

"That's what I been thinking about. Just trying to figure out how I'ma provide a better living for Lauren and the baby if she decides to have it."

"Having a child is a huge responsibility, Amari. Does your momma know?"

"Nah, I haven't mustered up the courage to tell her."

"Well, don't you think you need to let her know?"

"Yeah, but she's already going through a lot. I don't want to upset her any more. If we decide to keep the baby then I will let her know."

"You know you can't take too long, Mari. But listen baby, you know how grandma feel about them abortions. And you know I don't agree, but that's a decision you and Lauren have to make and I'm not gone tell you how to and what to do with your life. I trust that you'll make the right decision."

I sighed and took everything in. I had arrived at the point where life became real. It wasn't like being in high school, and stressing about finding a job to buy new clothes. My baby sister was in a coma and the love of my life was pregnant with a child we weren't sure we were ready to have. My dream of becoming a club owner seemed so unreachable. I had no idea where I was headed.

"I hear you grandma," I said no longer able to keep in the sadness and fear I held inside. I knew my grandma could read it all on my face.

"You hear me, but are you listening? You are a man now, Amari, so you're going to have to be strong like I know you can be. How is the club thing going?"

"It's going horrible. No one will give me a shot. I talked to about five different club owners around this area and most of them won't even listen to my ideas."

"Amari, you just got to stay at it. No one said it was going to be easy."

"I met with Reverend Wilson, and he has a friend that owns a club, and his friend is supposed to call me, but he hasn't called yet."

"Well, give the man some time, Amari."

"Grandma, it's been a week now. He should have been called me."

"You never know, Amari. I'm sure he's a very busy man, and he does own a club. You just have to think positive and be patient. Remember the night is darkest before dawn," grandma said.

"Maybe I'm just approaching it all wrong. Maybe this ain't for me. Maybe I ain't suppose to have that—"

Grandma cut me off. "Hush, Amari. Just hush. Don't go losing faith just because things are a little rough and hectic right now. All those successful people you look up to, you think everything was so easy for them? NO, it wasn't," grandma said angrily.

It was too much, I felt like running away. All I could do was close my eyes, put my head down and take a breath. My grandmother didn't like what she was seeing. "Mari, come have a seat right here."

I sat down next to her feeling like I was back in high school when I didn't make varsity my freshmen year.

"I know as a young black man in this world you have it hard. You got to pull that strength out. That strength is in your blood, baby; we come from strong people. I'm not gonna always be here and I need you to promise me, right here, right now, that you're not going to be a quitter. That you're going to do everything in your power to make sure you are in the position to take care of your mother, your sister, Lauren and that baby," grandma demanded.

I thought about what she said and I realized that there were so many other people my decisions affected.

"I promise, grandma. I promise." I didn't wanna upset her or myself for that matter. I intended to keep my word too. The mood settled and I got up to head inside to get something to drink.

"What time is it, Amari?"

"12:42."

"Oh shoot; I'm about to miss the Pick-It. Come walk with me to the store so I can play these numbers," grandma said.

"Grandma, why you always spending your money on that Lotto stuff? Isn't it just a waste of money?"

"Because, baby, when I hit tonight I'll be able to pay off these medical bills, help your momma out, get up out this area, and buy you your own club," grandma reasoned.

"Grandma, black people don't win that stuff. You got a better chance landing on Mars," I said.

"OK, and don't be all up in my face after I hit tonight, either," grandma said.

I laughed as we strolled down the block. It felt just like old times. Grandma been playing Pick-It as far back as I could remember. She always went in saying this will be her day to win. She never won, but she kept her faith, and I knew that it was that same faith that kept her sane through her lifetime of struggles. The sights and sounds were the same as they were when we walked to the store a few weeks ago: niggas on the corner, young girl pushing a stroller, and the same homeless lady outside. One of my old female friends called me over from the other side of the street. I hadn't spoken to her in a while so I walked over to see what was good with her.

"Ay grandma, I'll be right back, I'ma go say hi to an old friend across the street, I'll be right there in a minute," I said.

My grandma continued to walk to the store as I walked across the street to see Rasheeda.

"Well, well, well it's been awhile, Amari. What's up with you?"

She gave me a hug.

"Nothing much. What's going on with you?"

"I'm about to go home. I was just over here visiting my aunt before I head back to school."

"Oh, you still in school? I thought you graduated already."

"Yeah I did, I got my bachelors, but I'm going for my doctorate. I need it if I want to open my own Psychology firm."

"Oh you trying to get your own——"

Pop! Pop! Pop! Pop! A black Integra drove by and sprayed the whole corner with gunshots. I ducked and looked over to see if I could see my grandma. I was hoping she had gotten inside the store by now. She hadn't.

"Call the ambulance! Quick call somebody! Somebody help! Somebody help!" I was screaming for help. I had my cell phone in my holster, but I couldn't think straight.

Rasheeda used her phone to call the ambulance while I held grandma in my arms. "Grandma, stay with me. The paramedics are on their way. You gon' be just fine grandma. Just hold on, grandma. Please, grandma, just hold on."

After several moments, I heard sirens so I knew an ambulance was close by. I held grandma in my arms and prayed for God to save her.

"Grandma the ambulance is almost here: just hold on."

"Mari, baby, take care of my girls. Break the cycle, baby."

Tears rushing down my face, I promised my grandma again that I would hold the fort down. To this day I hear her last words in my head: "Mari, break the cycle, baby. Break the cycle."

She died in my arms, and I was furious. These niggas killed my grandma. Two other dudes got hit also. One got shot in the leg, and the other one in the arm, but my grandma wasn't so lucky. She got one in the chest, and one in the shoulder. I cried for the rest of that day, and many days after that. All I could think of was what my grandma said about breaking the cycle, and making sure everyone was taken care of. I loved my hood, I rep where I'm from proudly, but this hood ain't love me; this hood ain't love nobody. The hood doesn't have a heart, and it was time for me to change things. It was time for me to break the cycle, but a big part of me wanted to find out who killed grandma and break their neck.

Chapter Nine

We held the funeral for grandma, and a week went by, but I was so out of it I had no sense of time. Lauren was very supportive, but she was struggling also: she had been very close to grandma. I visited Sharea in the hospital every day. When I returned home, I typically turned on the TV and cried myself to sleep. I did have something to be excited about: although she wasn't fully recovered, Sharea had awakened from her coma. She would be up for a while and then she would go back to sleep for hours on hours and never say a word. I hadn't told her about grandma and I didn't know whether I should.

One day with a teddy bear and flowers in my hand, I headed to the hospital to see Sharea. To my surprise she was already up. The doctors had told me she was improving dramatically, but I wasn't expecting her to be sitting up and greeting me with a smile as I walked in.

"Hey brother," Sharea said in a feeble voice.

I gave her the get well gifts and said, "Hey, little sister. How are you feeling?"

"I don't know; I just feel tired and weak. What am I doing here, Amari? What happened to me?" Sharea slurred her words like she did the night Lauren and I had scooped her out of that party.

"Well, you were shot in the head, by accident, by your so-called boyfriend's cousin. Do you remember being with Dante, his cousin, and Cecily?" I asked

"I remember being at his house, but that's about it. He shot me, Amari? Oh my God," she said as she started to cry.

"Sha, it's okay. Don't cry. You're going to be fine. You were in a coma a few weeks but everything's going to be just fine," I said as I consoled her.

It had been a little over two weeks since grandma passed away, and I wrestled with whether to tell Sharea about it, but I figured the sooner I told her, the better.

"Sharea, I don't know how to tell you this, but grandma passed away," I said as I shed a tear.

She couldn't understand at first and after I repeated myself she burst into tears. I felt bad, but she had to find out someday. I prayed to God that He would get us through this hard time.

"How did she die, Amari?" she asked as I attempted to wipe the tears from her face.

"A drive-by over there where she always went to go play the Lotto at," I said.

"Well, did they catch the guys yet? Who did this, Amari?"

"Nah, I don't know who did it but I got my boys on it, Sharea, and I'ma find out. Don't even worry about that," I said.

I stayed with her until visiting hours were up. We talked about everything that had happened, and I tried to make her smile and lift her spirits, but the smiles didn't last too long. We both shed tears as we mourned our grandma. Hoping to change the mood, I told Sharea about Lauren's pregnancy. My sister was very excited by the possibility of becoming an auntie. She wanted us to keep the baby, and a big part of me wanted to as well. Lauren hadn't told me what she wanted to do, but I took it that she was leaning more towards having the abortion. Most women I knew who were having babies were more excited and looking at a bunch of baby stuff, but Lauren didn't get into all of that. She was very gung-ho on putting herself in the best possible situations so I knew that whatever decision she made, it was going to be a well-thought-out decision. The doctors came in as she was going to sleep.

"Doc, when do you think she will be able to come home?" I asked.

"Well, that all depends on her daily improvements. So far her speech has improved and she's beginning to display normal functioning. I would give her several more weeks," he said.

I wanted her home ASAP. The summer was almost over, we had missed out on the city carnival, and we had yet to go to Six Flags. That was our favorite place to go in the summer. At Six Flags, Sharea would beg me to play games and try my hand at winning stuffed animals for her, but she would also force me to go on roller coasters with her though she knew I was petrified of them. I felt so bad for her; Sharea wouldn't be able to start school in September like she wanted and she was so hyped about going to Rutgers. I prayed she would fully recover and be able to start school in January.

Sharea had fallen asleep so I left, went by to check on my moms, and then headed home to get some rest. My moms had taken my grandma's death pretty badly. She took some time off of work and spent several days stuck in bed. I talked with her and I brought over a few comedy movies to help lift her spirits.

It was a beautiful Saturday morning. I opened the blinds to let the sun in and then cooked breakfast for me and the misses. As Lauren and I sat at the table eating our buttermilk pancakes and bacon, I received a phone call. It was 9:30 in the morning and my boy Rahim was calling. I knew something had to be up for him to be calling that early.

"What the deal, Rah?" I said as I answered the phone.

"Yo, I just found out some good news."

"What news?"

"I know the niggas who killed your grandma," he said.

I stepped away from the table to get a little privacy from Lauren.

Walking into the bedroom I asked, "You do? Who was it? Where are they?"

"They from cross town, and I know the block they hang on. What you wanna do?"

"Come over to my spot," I said thinking of the revenge I was getting ready to get.

"Aight, my nigga, I'll be there in like forty-five," Rah said.

"Aight, call me when you outside."

I paused.

"And Rah...."

"Yeah?"

"Bring that thang," I said as we hung up the phone. I went back to the table to finish eating my breakfast.

"Who was that, Amari?" Lauren asked being nosy. I guess me walking away from the table made her a little suspicious.

"Rahim." I answered.

Lauren knew most of my friends and she knew what kind of a person Rahim was. Rahim had been my dude since high school and he was what most people would call a thug.

"What did he want?"

"Nothing, Lauren. Just man talk," I said. She stopped interrogating me and I hopped into the shower. As the water rained down on me, I thought about everything I wanted to do to the niggas that killed my grandma. My grandma ain't deserve to die. She never hurt anybody and those niggas gonna pay for what they did. As I got dressed, I noticed I had a missed call on my cell. I called the number to see who it was.

"Hello, did someone just call this number looking for Amari?" I asked.

"Yes, hello Amari. This is Elijah. Reverend Wilson told me you had some business ideas you wanted to share with me," he said.

"Oh yes, yes, I have several ideas that I think will be very beneficial for growing your business," I said excited to finally be receiving this call.

"Okay, well, can you be here in an hour?" he asked.

"An hour?" I paused for a moment. Rahim was on his way so we could go get the niggas that killed my grandma. There was no way I could do that and be dressed in time to meet with Mr. Elijah. What was I going to do? Should I accept the meeting with Mr. Elijah, the meeting I had been waiting desperately for? Or should I avenge my grandmother's death? I couldn't live with myself if I let them punks go without punishment.

"Yes, Amari. Is that going to be a problem? If so, we can reschedule for another time," he said.

I thought about what my grandma used to tell me all the time. She warned me that there would be times in my life when the wrong thing seemed more attractive then the right thing. That would be the moment during which my manhood would be tested.

"No, no, I should be able to meet with you in an hour. Where exactly would you like me to meet you?" I asked.

"Okay, well, my club is Club Fanatical, on the corner of Franklin and South Street in Orange. Is that far from you?" he asked.

"No, that's about a 20 minute ride."

"Okay, Amari, I will see you shortly."

We hung up the phone and my mind was far gone. I wanted badly to get the dudes that killed my grandma, but I had been waiting on that phone call for weeks. If I didn't take advantage of it now who knows when or if I would ever get the chance again? I had on a Polo tee, with some shorts, but I quickly changed into a suit. I thought about how I would present my ideas to Mr. Elijah. I didn't have a fancy PowerPoint display. I had nothing but raw thoughts. That would have to be enough: it was all or nothing. Rahim called and I looked out the window to see him pulling up. It was time for me to leave, so I headed for the door.

"Where are you going all dressed up, Amari?" Lauren asked.

"The club owner, who Reverend Wilson is friends with, just called me and wants me to meet him at his club right now."

"OH GREAT! Good luck, baby."

I walked out and went over to Rahim's car to let him know about the change of plans.

"Yo, what you doing wearing a suit, my dude? You tryna pop these niggas OG style, huh?"

"Yo Rah, I can't go through with it," I said.

"What you mean, nigga? These niggas killed your grandma," he reminded me as if I was unaware.

"I KNOW THAT, NIGGA, but this ain't how I get them back. It's 'bout time I break that cycle, Rah."

"Yo man, you bugging, kid," Rah said.

"Nah man, I got responsibility now. I got somewhere more important to be. I'll holla at you later, man. Go back home. I'ma come through later and chop it up with you," I said as I walked to get in my car.

When I arrived at Club Fanatical, Mr. Elijah was waiting right in the front.

"Hey, you must be Amari," he said.

"Yup, me in the flesh," I said as I shook his hand firmly.

We walked upstairs into his office and we talked about the different business ventures for which I had ideas. He seemed impressed, but he was more concerned about my purpose for getting into the business, and he wanted more insight into my motivation.

"What purpose do you think these ventures will serve?" Mr. Elijah asked.

"I just feel that many of my peers need that platform to really showcase their talent. I ride through my hood and I see a lot of people doing nothing with their lives, and just living with no hope. So with everything that I want to do with this club, I feel that I can change a lot of people's lives and give them that sense of fulfillment. So instead of that young boy slinging drugs on the corner, he can be at the club DJ'ing for one of the parties. For that young girl who has just had a baby, and feels her dream of becoming a fashion designer is over, she can have a place where she can showcase her fashion skills. And even if some of my peers might not have goals that include the use of this club, by seeing their friends or the people they grew up with doing something positive it might give them that belief that they can chase their dream in the same way," I said passionately.

"I like what I'm hearing," Mr. Elijah said nodding.

"Yeah, I just feel that we need that chance. We just need someone to give us an opportunity to show the world our passions as well as our skills. I believe I can be the man to help take care of that problem. It would also give your club a great reputation and produce good revenue while also giving back to the community," I said.

"You make some valid points, but why should I give you this opportunity, Amari? What is going to motivate you to come in here and work hard every day, whether things are going good or not so good?"

"I believe I should be given the opportunity because I'm hungry, I'm motivated and who better to give the opportunity than to an ambitious young man who wants to live out his dream? I have been through so much in recent months. I've been a casualty to the problem that I'm trying to fix. My grandma just got murdered in a drive-by. Those dudes didn't know my grandma, they weren't aiming at her, but they didn't have anything productive to do with their time. Her murder as well as the fact that I have a baby on the way fuels my desire to improve our culture. I feel I can get the job done."

"I'm sorry to hear about your loss and I understand exactly where you coming from," Mr. Elijah said.

"I just want that chance to change things for my family and do something that I have always dreamed of doing," I said.

"OK, I hear that. Now you say you have no college education; are you willing to go to school?" Mr. Elijah asked.

"Yes, sir, I'm willing to do anything," I said.

"Okay, if I hire you as my director of new ventures, what is your desired pay?" Mr. Elijah asked.

"I believe it should be solely on the money that I bring in to the club. I would love to start off with a 40% cut of whatever money I bring in," I said.

He looked down at his watch and I figured it was about time for this meeting to be over.

"OK, Amari, I love your ideas, I love your spirit and I love your cause. I will think hard about my decision and I will get back to you as soon as I decide what I want to do," Mr. Elijah said.

"Alright, no problem. Thank you so much," I said shaking his hand and leaving his office.

I felt good about our meeting. Mr. Elijah seemed to understand where I was coming from and he had to feel the drive I had to become successful. Then again, with my luck as it had been lately, I couldn't be sure.

I called Rahim to get the scoop on my grandma's killers and reported them to the cops. I figured I was paying my tax dollars for them to protect and serve so I might as well have them earn their keep. Rahim didn't like that idea too much, but there was no need to throw my life away. I had too much to live for.

Chapter Ten

The following week, Sharea was released from the hospital. Apparently she had recovered quicker than the doctors had expected. She wasn't 100 percent, and her head was still wrapped with a bandage, but she was able to walk with the assistance of a cane. Her speech was clear, but she took her time speaking. She was fighting for the return of a normal life, however normal it could be after suffering from such a tragic accident. She was such a warrior. My mother and I held a welcome home celebration at my grandmother's house. My mother had been laid off recently as a result of downsizing, and because my grandma's house was already paid off, ma moved in. I hoped she would take the initiative to open her babysitting service. The unemployment checks weren't going to last, and she deserved a job that she would enjoy doing. It was about time we all changed our lives. Sharea's friend Cecily phoned all of her friends, so when Sha came home, there were a gang of them in the backyard. It was going to be a big day in all our lives. My crazy uncle was on the grill cooking up the dogs and burgers, my aunts were getting drunk off the Jell-O shots, and my cousins were sitting at the table pity-patting it up, as my sister walked in. They all rushed over to give her hugs and kisses and ask her a zillion questions about everything that had went down. She was still in recovery so I made sure to let them know to be careful around her.

I knew the streets talked, but we all were surprised to see Sharea's boyfriend, Dante, show up to the cookout. I only resisted my urge to stomp his brains out because my sister said she would handle it.

"What are you doing here, Dante?" Sharea asked.

"I'm sorry about what happened, Rea. Do you forgive me?" Dante asked.

"No, I don't forgive you and you are not welcomed here in my house. WE ARE OVER DANTE!"

Dante tried to plead some more, but when my uncles gave him that look like they was about to fuck him up, he quickly exited the premises. Sharea walked over to me.

"Hey, Sha, I'm proud of you," I said.

"I'm sorry, Amari. You tried to warn me about hanging with him and it almost cost me my life. I wish I would have listened," Sharea said.

"It's okay, Sha. Now you know to listen to your big bruh. I ain't tryna spoil your fun, and I know you gonna date, but just take your time and be patient with making that decision on who you let into your life," I said.

"I will from now on, bruh," Sha said as she gave me a hug.

Everything settled down. We ate, we played cards, and we laughed at the little kids who were running around, going crazy, like they had just eaten a pound of sugar. I alerted everyone to gather around as I was about to make a toast. As everyone gathered, I noticed Reverend Wilson and saw that he had brought Mr. Elijah with him. I continued with my toast.

"I would like to toast to having my baby sister back home, where she belongs, and I want us to take a moment to thank God for blessing her with another chance at life," I said. We thanked the Lord during a moment of silence and then I continued with my announcement.

"OK, I have a big announcement to make. La La, can you come here, babe?"

"Yes, baby. What are you doing?" she asked as she approached me.

"Lauren, from day one, you always made me feel like I was the best man on earth. You've always supported me, and even when things were rough, you never gave up on me. Even to this day, I know I haven't been the perfect boyfriend for you, and I've made my mistakes, but I want you to know that I'm trying. I'm trying very hard to be the best man I can possibly be."

"Baby, you are the best," Lauren said as she cut in.

"We've been together for almost five years now, and I know you've been thinking about whether or not you want to keep our baby."

My mother interrupted me, "BABY! What baby, Amari?"

"Ma, just let me finish," I said before continuing.

"As I was saying, La La, I want you to know that I'm ready to be a father, and I'm even more ready to be your husband," I said as I bended down on one knee.

"La La, will you marry me?"

Tears, which I assumed were tears of joy, ran down into Lauren's beautiful smile.

"Yes, baby. Yes, I will marry you and I want to have your baby," she answered as she jumped into my arms.

Everyone clapped and my mother started to cry. Reverend Wilson interrupted the applause, "I would like to thank God, once again, for healing Sharea and I want us all to congratulate Amari and Lauren on their engagement, but that is not the only big news of today. Amari, do you remember when I told you I needed you to do something for me for the church Youth Foundation?"

"Yes, I remember, Rev. What's going on?" I asked.

"Well, how would you like to coordinate the Youth Foundation's First Annual Talent Show?"

"Sure Rev, I don't have a problem with that. Are we going to have it at the church? "I asked.

"No, Amari, not unless the new director of new ventures for Club Fanatical wants to host all of his events at the church. I don't think Elijah will be too happy with that," Reverend Wilson said laughing.

Mr. Elijah started to laugh and said, "Amari, I would have to agree with my old friend on that one."

Then it hit me. "Oh so, I got the…I got the… I got the position?" I asked barely able to get the words out of my mouth.

"Yes, Amari. You remind me of myself when I was your age, young and ambitious, and I would love to have you as my partner," Mr. Elijah answered.

"Oh my God! I can't believe it. Thank you! Thank you!" I said as I shook his hand.

"But, there is one condition," Mr. Elijah said.

"What's the condition?"

"You have to take some college courses, so you can improve your business savvy and better yourself," Mr. Elijah said.

"OK, Mr. Elijah, no problem."

"Alright, so we are going to celebrate today, but tomorrow I want you to come to the club so we can discuss the details."

"Okay, you got it, sir," I said.

I felt so happy, but yet so sad. I had my sister back home, a baby on the way, and a beautiful fiancé, but my grandma wasn't here to see it. I was finally becoming the man she wanted me to be. I was breaking the cycle she feared I would fall into and she wasn't here to enjoy it with me. Still, I felt like this was the beginning of a new life, a better life, and that was exactly what this family needed. We had been through so much this summer, and it was about time something good happened to us. I sat on the front porch thinking about everything that had transpired. I didn't have my own club yet, but I was a partner and I knew that in due time I would open my own spot. I wondered about the sex of my baby, and I imagined how marriage would change my relationship with Lauren. Lauren was such an angel, so I was certain it wouldn't be too bad. I had learned so much and it was time for me to make that change my grandmother so desperately wanted. It was time I let her live through me, and as I took advantage of my new capacity as a partner, grandma and I would help transform victims to victors. My mother touched me on my shoulder and broke me out of my trance.

"Amari, we ran out of ice, so I need you to go to the store and pick up some. Oh, and bring some of those Icy Pops back for the kids," moms said.

"Aight, ma."

It was a little further, but I walked to the store in the opposite direction of the store where my grandma was murdered. It had only been about a month since she passed and I was having a hard time getting the images from that day out of my head. I wasn't ready to go back to the old spot.

I saw a few guys I had grown up with. I looked around and noticed how nothing had changed since I was a little kid. Some of the boys had grown facial hair, the girls had become mothers (and grown a little fatter), but that was about it. I walked into the store and got the Icy Pops for the kids and the ice for my mother. As I walked out of the store, I bumped into Darryl, one of the boys that had graduated with Sharea.

"What's up, my G?" he said to me.

"What's going on, kid? How you?" I asked.

"I'm living man: trying to stay out of jail," he replied as he lifted the black and mild out of his mouth.

"I hear you, man. That should be an easy thing, though," I said.

"Nah man, it's hard out here. These cops be buggin, my G," he said taking another pull.

"Well, let me ask you this: what do you want to do with your life? What are you seventeen, eighteen now?" I asked.

"Yeah, I'm seventeen."

"Well, have you thought about college, or what you want to do?" I asked.

"Nah, I ain't really think too much of it. No one in my family ever did the college thing. My pops been locked up for about seven years now and my moms is an office assistant. I just been hustling these rocks for some ends. You feel me? My little sisters and brothers gotta eat," he said.

"I feel you. I ain't have my pops either, but nah man, you gotta find another way."

"Find another way? Nigga, there ain't no other way," Darryl said.

"Man, listen; I want you to think about something. Your pops ain't there, and your moms is home struggling to take care of you. No one in your family ever became what they wanted to become. But that doesn't mean you have to be just like them. So while you walking home, while you playing your XBOX or smoking that weed with your friends, I want you to think hard about what you are doing to break your cycle," I said.

"Break my cycle?" he asked looking puzzled, sort of how I looked when my grandma told me the same thing.

"YES, BREAK YOUR CYCLE…."

info@marquisewatson.com

Marquise T. Watson
1333 Sloane Blvd , Plainfield NJ 07060
(973) 986-2576

www.marquisewatson.com   info@marquisewatson.com

Item	Unit Price	Quantity	Amount
"Break The Cycle"	$12.95		$
	Subtotal		
	Shipping & Handling $1.50 per item		
	Total		$

Payment by: ☐ Check or money order made payable to Marquise T. Watson
    Credit Card   ☐ Visa   ☐ M/C   ☐ Discover   ☐ AMEX
Card # _____   Exp. Date _____
Signature: _____
Name: _____
Address: _____
City _____   State _____   Zip _____

Marquise T. Watson
1333 Sloane Blvd , Plainfield NJ 07060
(973) 986-2576

www.marquisewatson.com   info@marquisewatson.com

Item	Unit Price	Quantity	Amount
"Break The Cycle"	$12.95		$
	Subtotal		
	Shipping & Handling $1.50 per item		
	Total		$

Payment by: ☐ Check or money order made payable to Marquise T. Watson
    Credit Card   ☐ Visa   ☐ M/C   ☐ Discover   ☐ AMEX
Card # _____   Exp. Date _____
Signature: _____
Name: _____
Address: _____
City _____   State _____   Zip _____

info@marquisewatson.com